To Love the Broken & Unhealed

L L MOMON

Dedication

To every woman who has faced trauma and still found the strength to rise
This is for you
For the nights you cried in silence, the days you wore a brave face
and the battles no one else saw
You are living proof that healing is possible
and your presence in this world is not only needed but deeply cherished
You are worthy. You are loved. You belong here

Love and embrace yourself fiercely, including the parts of you that you haven't met yet.

L.L. Momon

Trigger Warning

To Love the Broken & Unhealed contains themes that may be distressing to some readers. Including offensive language, emotional, physical, and sexual abuse, trauma, mention of suicide, violence, and mental health struggles. The first two chapters are **extremely heavy** but I encourage you to hold on. It gets better. I promise.

This story explores the raw and painful journey of what healing often looks like after trauma. While it also speaks to resilience, love, and survival, please prioritize your well-being as you read.

If you find any part of this story difficult, it's okay to take a break. You are not alone.

Synopsis

Seventeen-year-old Gigi Parker has only known pain. She has been used by her mother, abused by men, and forced to grow up far too soon. One violent night changes everything, and she's thrust into the streets with nothing but a duffle bag and a dream of freedom.

When a late-night run-in with a masked stranger turns into an unexpected lifeline, Gigi finds herself in the care of Echo. A young man with his own haunted past and a heart big enough to hold them both. In his home, she finds something she's never known...peace.

But healing doesn't come easy. As Gigi fights to reclaim her power and future, she'll have to confront everything she's tried to escape. Because love, real love, doesn't come without scars.

To Love the Unhealed is a raw, gritty, and redemptive coming of age love story about trauma, survival, and the quiet power of genuine care. L.L. Momon delivers an unforgettable story of pain, healing, and the kind of love that doesn't demand perfection, only truth.

To Love the Broken & Unhealed

L.L. MOMON

Chapter One

FEBRUARY-2015

At 11:11 p.m., just as I'd drifted off to sleep, there was a knock at the front door.

I froze. At first, I told myself to ignore it. It was probably somebody at the wrong house. But the knock came again, even louder this time. Harder. Almost frantic. Then it turned into pounding.

Boom. Boom. Boom.

I laid there, eyes wide open, heart racing. *Who the hell is that?* I waited, hoping they'd take the hint and get the hell on. But whoever it was wasn't leaving. They were knocking like they had a damn warrant.

I threw the covers off, irritated and half on edge, and stormed out of bed. My feet shuffled across the cold floor as I headed to my mama's room.

I peeked in...she was under the covers, fan on blast,

knocked out like nothing in the world was happening. Typical. I pulled her door shut and made my way to the front.

When I yanked the door open, Rolla stormed in without so much as a hello, brushing past me with the kind of heat you could feel before he even said a word.

“Where in the fuck is yo mama?” he barked. “I know that bitch ain’t sleep. I just got off the phone with her less than ten minutes ago.”

I blinked, caught off guard. “Rolla, I just checked. She’s in bed with her head under the covers, fan going. That usually means she’s out for the night.”

“Whatever, Gigi. I’m going back there. Me and her got business to handle.”

I shrugged and waved him off. I’d seen this kind of late-night drama before. My mama was no stranger to people showing up unannounced. I was used to it.

Still, something about tonight felt... off.

I climbed back into bed and shoved my earbuds in, letting the music drown out the rest of the world. But the peace didn’t last long. My bedroom door creaked open. I didn’t move. I didn’t even breathe. Maybe if I stayed still, he’d get the hint.

He didn’t.

“Get up, Gigi,” Rolla growled, voice lower now, but

sharp. "Yo mama was supposed to talk to you before I got here. I need you to get your ass up. Now!"

A chill ran through me as he yanked the covers away from my body. He began tugging at my shorts.

Frantic, I screamed. "Stop, Rolla, please," but he didn't. Instead, he slapped my face so hard that my jaw rocked.

"Now shut the fuck up and take those damn shorts off, Gigi! I'm not trying to be here all night long. I've got shit to do in the morning."

"No, I'm not taking anything off because I'm not doing shit with you or anybody else, Rolla. You can fight me all you want, but the last time was the last time. I'm serious. I refuse to stay another day in this raggedy-ass house, being forced to fuck on old, no-good niggas like you."

"No good? Girl, who the hell are you talking to? It can't be me. And who the fuck are you to judge? Your mama been whoring for years."

Grabbing the covers, I pull them tightly to shield my body, I said firmly, "My mama might be a whore, but that has nothing to do with me. She's foolish enough to do whatever you want, but I'm not her. So please, get the fuck out of my room, Rolla."

"Yeah, yeah. Talk that shit all you want, lil' girl, but I ain't going nowhere. What you need to do is un-ass those draws before you fuck around and piss me off. And I know you don't want that," he grunted, lowering his eyes at me as he inched closer.

I shot back, "I'm not un-assing anything. It's not a good time, and I'm not feeling well, Rolla. Plus, I've got school tomorrow, so this is gonna have to wait."

"I didn't drive all the way over here to argue with your ass, Gigi. I already gave your mama ten perks, a gram of that pure, and a hundred dollars for you."

"And? What's that supposed to mean?"

"Stop playing dumb. You know exactly what it means."

"Nothing to me!! Whatever deal you and my mama worked out ain't got shit to do with me," shrugging, I rolled over to face the wall.

"It means I'm not leaving without getting some pussy or my shit back. And we both know your mama popped three of them perks as soon as I gave them to her. Then the sorry bitch gave me the hundred dollars back for five more, so she ain't got that either. And the blow? Gone. I can hear her slicing lines across that old-ass nightstand of hers right now. So yeah...looks like you're shit outta luck."

Trying to stall, I pleaded, "Rolla, you know my mama's sick on that shit. She doesn't make the best choices when she's high. She probably doesn't even realize what time of the month it is. Whatever arrangement she made with you will have to wait. I'm on my period. We can't do this tonight."

It was a lie, but I was desperate.

"Gigi, I'm a grown-ass man. What does a period have to do with anything?" He asked while grunting and rubbing the small bulge growing in his jeans.

"It's disgusting, that's what. Why would you want somebody else's blood and insides on you? It's my blood, and even I can't stand the smell. So why would you want that?"

At this point, I'd say anything to keep him away. I didn't even have a cycle. My mama put me on birth control at fifteen, and I only got my period every six months. But of course, I kept that to myself.

"Please, just leave. Get out, Rolla!" I begged. "I'll take care of you when my period's over. I swear. I'll have Mama call you and you can come back. I'll do all the nasty shit you like but not tonight."

"Gigi, you must think I'm some kind of fool. I told you already. I'm not leaving until I get what I paid for. That pussy and that pretty lil' mouth. Your mama said I had an hour to do what I want with you and I'm not leaving till that hour's up. Just so you know, it don't start until you do. I don't give a fuck about a period. All bitches bleed. You ain't the first and you won't be the last. So go get some towels or something so you don't mess up this nice-ass bedspread."

I looked around the room, hoping to find something to defend myself with. But my room was damn near barren. All I had was a chair, window fan, and a small-ass lamp that wouldn't do shit but piss him off if I hit him with it.

I stared at him. He was serious. But so was I.

I had bear mace, but if I sprayed him, I'd catch it too in my small-ass room.

A knife I'd stolen from one of Mama's tricks was hidden under my pillow. I thought about stabbing him, but I didn't want to kill him and end up in jail. I just wanted him gone.

Then I remembered the small baseball bat under my bed.

He was watching me like a hawk, but I refused to be prey again. If I was gonna get out of this, I had to think fast.

Grumbling, I muttered, "Alright then, Rolla. Damn." I sucked my teeth while silently plotting. "I swear on my granny's grave. This is the last time I'm doing this. I'll give you head first, then we can fuck. Let's just get this shit over with so I can shower and go to sleep."

Rubbing the imprint in his pants, he smiled wide.

"Now *that's* what the fuck I'm talking about, Gigi. That's what type of time I'm on."

As he stood to unbutton his pants, I kneeled in front of him while pretending to place my hair in a bun. While he was preoccupied with trying to rare back to reach under his big ass pot belly to find his button, I reached under the bed to get a good grip on the bat.

As soon as I heard his zipper slide, I came up swinging with the strength of my ancestors. Cracking him right in the ribs, he wretched and screamed in agony.

"Ayyyyyy, lil bitch. What the fuck is wrong with you?" he grumbled, as he ducked and ran around the room. "I'm serious Gigi, put that damn bat down before I fuck you up. Ayyyyy Shanice, you better come and get this lil bitch," he yelled. "She's in here swinging this bat like she has lost her damn mind."

MY MAMA BURST into the room and charged straight towards me. "Gigi, put that damn bat down and do what he tells you. Stop fucking around. I am sick and tired of going through this shit with you. Just do it and get it over with."

Shifting my stance, I voiced, "No, I'm not putting shit down. I've got school tomorrow and I just want to go to bed. I should be in here asleep. Not in here running from his ass!! I don't know why you would send him in here anyway."

"Why do you think I gave you a couple shots of Paul Masson and a half a pill? I gave it to you so that you could relax, Gigi. I told you that you only had to do this a little while longer and then you could stop. Now go on and give Rolla what he came here for. Do it for your mama please," she said as she attempted to grab my hand.

Snatching away, I let in on her. "Mama, I'm not doing shit for you! Hell, if you care so much about him being satisfied, why don't you suck his stanky ass dick then. This is what you do. Not me." I said as I gently laid the bat across my shoulder blade.

"It will only take you a couple of minutes, Gigi. It's not the worst thing in the world."

I snapped my neck around so fast that it almost flew off my shoulders. "What do you mean it's not? It is to me. These niggas don't even care enough to bathe their asses before they come over here. I will never get used to the cigarette, liquor filled breath and musty nuts. The thought of it makes me want to throw up all over myself just to keep them from touching me, but these sick bastards would probably get off on that too. You can let Tom, Dick, and Harry turn you every which way but loose if you want. I'm not doing shit else with these filthy, sick and demented, pedophile, child raping ass niggas ever again."

Chapter Two

"Now, hold the fuck on, Gigi. You are not going to stand here in my face, in my house, and disrespect me. I'm still your mama and you will do what I tell you to do."

"I'm not trying to disrespect you, Mama. I'm just letting you know that I'm not doing it."

"Look, Gigi, I'm the one who takes care of you. I put food in your mouth and clothes on your back. You're seventeen and not a baby anymore. You need to realize that ain't shit in this world free, and it's time for you to start contributing to this household." She sniffled and rubbed her nose. I could always tell when she'd been snorting powder. Her nose ran constantly, and she couldn't stop touching it. It was disgusting.

"Mama, are you being serious right now? Do you

really think that this is helping me in any kind of way? Do you think that this is what teaching me responsibility looks like? Because it's not. What it is doing is keeping those pills and little baggies on your nightstand and a little change in your pocket. That's all it's doing."

Pissed off, she snapped, "You need to watch your mouth, little bitch, and watch how you talk to me. What I do behind closed doors is my business."

"You make it my business by making me do shit like this. Especially if I'm helping to fund your habit. I don't benefit from this in any kind of way."

"Yes, you do baby. You do benefit from it. You just don't see it now, but you will in time. Especially when you get older and have to take care of yourself." Shanice retorted.

"Mama, if sucking dick and fucking these demented ass niggas is your idea of an afterschool job, then you are sicker than I thought. How about letting me babysit or do hair, nails or something constructive. I'd even be happy working at McDonalds. Pleasing and getting abused by these men isn't teaching me shit but how to be a whore like you."

She raised her hand to hit me, but I wasn't taking that shit tonight. I stopped her by grabbing her wrist as we stood eye to eye. Although she didn't say it, I knew that she could feel that it wasn't going down the way it usually did.

I'd never put my hands on my mother and never intended to because my grandmother taught me that not honoring your parents would shorten your days. So, I usually cowered down and let her throw her fits but tonight I would fight her like a bitch in the street if she or anyone else in this house put their hands on me. I was DONE!

Standing in the corner of the room, Rolla spat. "Shanice!! Now I know damn well that you are not going to sit up here and let this lil bitch talk to you like that. You need to put your foot down and make her do what we talked about, or you and I are going to have a problem. You're the Mama, right? Act like it!!! I wish one of my daughters would talk to me crazy like that. I'd hit the little bitch in her mouth."

"Rolla, why don't you shut the fuck up and let me handle my child the way I see fit, please," she snapped, turning to me and trying to inject some authority into her voice. "You better watch your fucking mouth when you're talking to me. Like I said, I'm still your mama. You act like I don't love and care about you."

"Because you don't," I scoffed, backing into the corner of my room, opposite the one Rolla was slumped in.

"I do love you, Gigi. But you need to know how the

real world works. I don't want you walking out those doors thinking you can just show your pretty face and get what you want. These men out here are not going to take care of you and give you what you need if you aren't satisfying them. Whether you realize it or not, you're learning a very valuable skill here. This is a way to make sure your needs are met, and you get the things you want."

I sucked my teeth in disbelief that someone, especially my mother, could actually think like this. It had to be the drugs.

"First off, Mama, this is not love. I don't know what kind of sick shit you've got going on in your mind, but this ain't it. Second, I will not rely on men the way you have. You do all of this, and your quality of life hasn't improved at all. I don't ever want a man to take care of me. Fuck them. I'd rather work an honest job and make my own money than depend on them."

Smacking her lips, she cut in, "Gigi, you're talking crazy. That's hustling backwards, baby. I'm not about to work nobody's job slaving for ten dollars an hour when I can get a man to get it for me."

"Damn a man," I barked. "These men ain't shit. How you don't see that after all these years is crazy to me. I'm only seventeen and I can already see that they're all the same. Only a few things matter to them: sex, head, and money. I want more out of life than this. I'm your child.

You should want better for me. Instead, you're running me into the ground," I said somberly.

Cupping my chin, she muttered, "I'm not running you into shit. I'm trying to teach you the game. How to hustle and use what you got."

"No thank you. I'll pass. Because you are in no position to teach anyone anything. You're a walking tragedy." She turned her head away from me, trying not to make eye contact. But I could tell the truth stung. It needed to be said, so I continued. "You have no education, no money, no morals, no integrity, no man. Just tricks and drugs. You do all this hustling and we still live at the bottom of the barrel.

You were right about one thing; you *have* taught me some very valuable things."

"I know I did. Shiddd, baby. Thank you for giving me credit for something," she said proudly, standing there smoking her cigarette and tapping her bare foot against the concrete floor.

"Yes, you've taught me what *not* to do. You've taught me exactly what I *don't* want out of life. Look at the disgusting and vile things you have me doing. I would never treat my children the way you treat me. Never. Because I will want better for them, like you should want for me!"

Before she could respond, Rolla interrupted, pissed

off. "Heyyy, heyyy, *heyyy*! Can you two bitches stop arguing and take care of me? I don't wanna hear all this shit. Talk it out after I leave."

"He's right. Gigi, please stop with this Hallmark bullshit. You can do better another day, but for now I need you to take care of Rolla or you can get the fuck out of my house. I'm tired of your mouth anyway. You're so ungrateful, and you act like your life is all bad. If you ask me, we're living pretty good."

"Good? You call this good? The rats and roaches. The toilets that don't work. The water and lights that are barely on. That empty-ass refrigerator. Do you even realize I've been wearing the same clothes for three years? I've been telling you for months about everything going wrong in this house. But you don't seem to hear anything except that expired credit card slicing those lines and that pill bottle shaking. It's like nothing else matters to you. Those drugs are your God. The *only* God you'll listen to."

"You know what, Gigi? *Get out.* Get the fuck outta my house!" she screamed. "Since you hate it here so bad and you think you can do better than me, take your ass out there in them streets and try to get it on your own. I guarantee you'll be back in less than a week. It's hard out there, girl. Go on and see for yourself."

Looking down her nose at me, she grabbed Rolla's hand and left the room, slamming the door behind her.

I rushed to my bed, raised the mattress, and pulled out the $600 I'd been saving for months. I grabbed my little duffle bag and stuffed it until it couldn't hold anything else. I made sure to get my book-bag. I had a huge math test the next day that I refused to fail. Throwing on my coat, I grabbed my knife, bear mace, and phone. I slid on my shoes and headed out the door.

I didn't know where I was going or what I was going to do. But I *did* know one thing for damn sure, living under a bridge would've been better than living in that fuckery.

About half a mile from my mama's house was a corner store. I walked in that direction and sat down on the bench outside. I *should* have been scared out of my mind, but there wasn't an ounce of fear in me. My adrenaline was rushing, and my heart was pounding out of my chest.

But for the first time in years...I felt free.

Chapter Three

In times like these, I wished my granny was around. She would have never let this type of shit go on. She knew my mama wasn't doing right by me, so she protected me at all costs. Mainly by keeping me away from that house. Most of our time was spent at church functions or just out and about, visiting the sick and shut in which I enjoyed. The wisdom from the elders wasn't anything that you could read in a book so like the nerd I was, I soaked it up.

My grandmother did everything possible to keep me from going down the same path that my mother did. My mama was too far gone, and my granny knew it. She'd given up hope of saving her from the streets, but she did her best to save me from being like her. My granny could see the men starting to lust and stare at me.

Since I was a baby, I'd been told that I was beautiful. I had big, doe like eyes with long eyelashes, long curly tresses, dimples, smooth chocolate skin and I was naturally curvy to boot. It got worse when I hit puberty because my ass and titties spread like butter. There was nothing anyone could do about that though. It was hereditary. My grandma passed down her shape and looks to my mama and my mama to me.

Granny always hid her shape because she said that men couldn't see past it. She wanted to be known for what was on the inside, not the outside. She taught me the same. Not my mama, she loved the attention that it brought her, and she didn't possess an ounce of modesty. She loved being ogled over.

The good qualities that I have, came from my granny. She gave me so many life lessons and she taught me how to watch out for myself. Granny was my shield from all this bullshit. A sudden heart attack took her away from this world and my life had been in shambles ever since.

As I sat reminiscing about my granny, the adrenaline faded. It was only then that it dawned on me that it was cold as hell on that bench and I was developing a bad case of the cottonmouth. I shook off my thoughts and delayed coming up with a masterplan to go and quench my thirst.

Snatching up my belongings, I strolled into the store to get a bottle of water. As I grabbed the bottle from the cooler, I found myself in the middle of an armed robbery. Two gun-toting men wearing ski mask were holding the clerk at gunpoint and I was thinking that this day couldn't get any shittier. At that point I was numb and tired of people and their bullshit. I didn't give a damn if they pulled the trigger or not. All I asked is that they made it quick.

Disregarding the robbery, I casually sashayed past the gunman and walked up to the counter. He pushed me to the side, his eyes piercing my soul as he yelled his demands to the cashier.

"Empty the muthafucking register and don't try any funny shit either or she will be your last customer."

The clerk did as he was told and put all the money from the register in a paper sack.

Looking at me directly in the eyes, the gunman urged me to get out of his way. "Don't you see that I'm in the middle of robbing this muthafucka. You must have a death wish or something. I should blow your shit back right now for just walking up on me like that," he barked.

"Oh, my bad," I casually shrugged, as I placed three dollars on the counter and walked out of the store. Even with his mask on, I could tell that he was watching me through the door as I adjusted my belongings. Disappearing from his sight, I took off down the street. As I trekked up the road, I called my homegirl Tasia to ask if I could stay at her house for the night.

"Tasia, I'm sorry for waking you up but I was wondering if it was ok if I came over. Me and Mama got into it again and I need somewhere to stay for the night."

"Girl yes. Come on. It's like 1:00 in the morning and my mama is asleep. She won't know that you are here, and we will be gone to school before she gets up. Gigi, how are you going to get here?"

"Don't worry about that," I griped out of frustration. "Just unlock the door and I'll slide through in a little bit."

As I'm speaking to her, a car crept past me at a snail's pace. It stopped, then backed up.

"Hey lil mama, do you need a ride? Where are you going?" A voice yelled out the driver side of a brand new 2015 jet black Hellcat SRT. It was dark, so I was definitely not about to get in the car with two strange men.

"No thank you. I'm straight. My friend lives right up the street, so I don't need a ride." I said as I began to pick up the pace.

"Girl, I know a lie when I hear one. Don't tell me that you are scared. Your ass wasn't scared back there at that store. Not walking in front of a loaded gun you're not."

As I looked up, I recognized his eyes from the store. They were as beautiful as he was. Now that he didn't have the mask on, I could see him clearly and he was gorgeous.

He was a tall, athletic built redbone with a short caesar fade, a short goatee and skin as smooth as butter.

Putting my head back down, I continued walking. He put the car in park and jumped out. Startling me, I almost took off running. Noticing the fear in my eyes, he tried to deter it by saying, “Don’t worry Lil Thugger. I’m not going to do anything to you. I just want to talk to you.”

“Talk to me? Like you were talking to that clerk back there. No thanks, I’m good,” I quipped as I stood there with a straight face.

“Listen, I know that what happened back there looked fucked up, but it’s not what you thought it was.”

“Look, I didn’t see shit, I don’t know shit and I don’t want any problems. If you are worrying about me saying anything. Don’t. This is the hood, and niggas get robbed every day. It’s a regular occurrence around here. If you hadn’t noticed, I mind my business and drink water,” I remarked, as I held up the water bottle and took a swig.

“Well damn, it’s like that? A nigga can’t even get a conversation with you?”

“I’m not trying to be rude, but it’s like 1 in the morning and you just robbed a man at gunpoint in front of me. I’m tired, hungry and I just want to get to my friend's house so that I can go to bed. I have school in the morning and I need to at least get a couple of hours of rest.”

"Come on, get in. I'll take you wherever you want to go. It's too late for you to be walking out here by yourself. This town is full of crazies. Plus, I know you are lying about your friend being up the street. There's nothing up the street but liquor stores and pawn shops. Where are you really going?"

"Damn, you nosy as hell. She lives on Gautier street if you just gotta know."

"Gautier street? Girl, that is almost across town. If you don't get your ass in this car and let me give you a ride. It will take you two hours to get there on foot. Not to mention the bridge that you have to walk across. I promise you that nothing will happen to you. Just get in," he urged.

Screaming from the passenger side of the car, his homeboy yelled out the window, "Man fuck that bitch. If her stupid ass want to stay out here in the cold and walk six miles, then let her. We need to bounce."

Pissed at his words, I advised, "You need to check your homeboy because I don't play that calling me out my name shit. I've had enough of that for a lifetime. I will not let him or another nigga on this earth talk to me like that ever again and that's on everything that I love."

"Ayyyyye Jah, chill out man. Don't be calling Lil Thugger out her name."

"Forreal though. It's cold as shit. Either you are

swerving or not. This is your last chance cause we've got to bounce."

"Ok, I'll come but just know that I've got a weapon and some bear mace, and I'm not scared to use it."

He laughed as he went around to the passenger door and told his homeboy to get in the backseat. Jah did, begrudgingly of course, and motioned for me to get in. He put my bags in the backseat, and we slid off.

Chapter Four

"So, whats your name Lil Thugger? I'm Echo, and before you ask, yes that's my real name."

"I'm Genevieve. Everyone calls me Gigi."

"Gigi huh. I've never met anyone your age named Genevieve."

"I know, I was named after my granny. Nice to meet you, Echo. I wish it was under better circumstances but God's timing right?"

"Ion know about all that but if you say so," he shrugged.

"What do you not know about? Do you not believe in God?"

"Actually, I do. I was raised up in church. I believe in God, I just don't know if I believe everything in the bible."

"Whatever you say. I have no heaven or hell to put you

in, so I can't judge. Listen, I know I said that I need to get somewhere and sleep but is there any way that we can stop and get something quick to eat. I'm starving. I haven't eaten a bite all day and don't worry, I can pay for my own meal."

"Aye man, y'all can take me home then. I got food at the crib and after hitting that lick, I'm trying to be out the streets," Jah mumbled.

"I got you. I'm gonna go ahead and drop you off and Lil Thugger and me gonna hit up the Wafflehouse."

Echo whipped his Dodge Hellcat as if he'd been driving it his whole life. Within minutes we arrived at a well-lit, gated community. I wasn't easily surprised, but when Jah said drop me off at home, a place like this was the last thing that I'd imagined. They dapped each other up as he climbed from the backseat and walked up to a two-story mansion with a horseshoe shaped driveway. Sliding his key in the door, he disappeared from our sight.

We pulled off in silence and I was confused. I didn't want to be nosey, but dammit I couldn't help it. I turned to Echo and inquired. "Why in the world are y'all robbing places when your boy lives in a place like this? Is this how he afforded this house? Robbing people? Are y'all stick up kids or something?"

"Nawl Gigi, it's not what you think. I told you back there at the store that it wasn't like that. I guess you thought I was lying. Enough of all that. You said you were hungry right? Let's fix that."

We pulled into the Wafflehouse parking lot and he killed the motor. Getting out the car, he jogged around to my side and opened my car door again. Me not being used to this kind of treatment, I was taken aback a little. He seemed like the perfect gentleman but less than 30 minutes ago, I watched him put a gun to the clerk's face and then threaten to peel my shit back.

Yet with me, he was just as kind as ever. I tell you, men are definitely the confusing ones. I hopped out the hellcat and we made our way into the Waffle House. I smiled at the waitress and took a seat in the corner as I've always done and he followed. Instead of sitting across from me, he sat beside me, and my skin began to crawl from the closeness.

With a smile, I muttered, "Echo, I don't mean to be rude, but could you sit over there? I haven't eaten all day remember and I am going to need all the arm room that I can get."

Getting up, he winked his eye and sat across from me. I breathed a sigh of relief.

"Is this better, Lil Thugger?"

"Yes, it is but why do you keep calling me that? I told you that my name was Gigi."

"Anybody who walks in front of a loaded gun and

stands there like they don't have shit to lose, has to be a thug. If you are not, you could have fooled me."

"If you knew the day that I had you would understand. At that moment, I didn't give a shit. I just wanted some water and to go on about my business. I hate to be so intrusive, but please explain to me what just happened because your boy lives in a fucking mansion for goodness sake, and y'all are out here hitting up corner stores. Make it make sense."

"Intrusive huh. I see that someone paid attention in school."

"What are you trying to insinuate? I'm not a dummy. I'm a straight A student and I have the highest grade point average in my class."

"Damn, that's dope" Echo chimed, "I should've stayed my ass in school. I didn't do half bad myself, but I let these dumb ass street niggas talk me into dropping out. Honestly, I regret that shit til this day."

As he talked about his experiences in school, I couldn't help but notice the shape of his slanted eyes, his thick eyebrows and his long lashes. I marveled at the freckles that sprawled across his nose and those big juicy lips that would cost a good three G's in Beverly Hills. As I admired how handsome this brother was, the waitress arrived and took our order.

I asked for cheese eggs and grits with bacon, a pecan

waffle and an apple juice. He told the waitress to bring him the same.

"Back to the school thing. You do realize that it isn't too late right? You can always go take your GED and in our state, it comes with a high school diploma. It would be like you never left at all," I advised.

"Seriously? I never knew that. Good looking out. I'm going to look into it. I'm sure that will make my Mama proud. Everyone else in my family has their diplomas and went off to college. I'm the only one that hasn't done shit really. That's gonna change though because I've got a plan."

"Before we talk about this plan, can we talk about what happened back there at that store? That shit is really bothering me because that man looked like he was going to shit on himself."

"Gigi, trust me. He was cool. He is a homeboy of mine and it was an inside job. That nigga hates his boss. He found out that he'd been cheating him out of his money, so he came up with the plan to rob him. He told me about it, and I offered to help because I need bread too. Shidd, I talked to Jah and he was down, so we robbed his ass. My homeboy and I will split the money two ways."

"Only two ways? It was three of y'all. Why only two?"

"Because you see where my boy lives at. He doesn't

need that little ass chump change. He just went with me for back up."

"Oh, OK, I get it. That makes sense."

"Now, since we are telling our truths, why were you at a corner store this time of morning? Especially when you have school tomorrow. And how old are you? Sorry for all of the questions, but I'm just intrigued by you. What's your deal?"

I'd never been very good at lying, so I didn't. Instead of giving him a rundown of what happened earlier. I told him that I was seventeen and that I was scheduled to graduate from high school in three months. Explaining that my mother and I had a disagreement. It turned ugly and as a result, she put me out. End of story.

There was no way that I was about to divulge that my mother was a prostitute and an addict that had me turning tricks to support her raging drug habit. I'm usually against half-truths, but I think some occasions called for it. This was one of them. Besides, I didn't need him judging me because I was not my mother.

As I told my truths, he in turn told his. He was nineteen, soon to be twenty. He worked at the Jiffy Lube in town, and he dreamed of one day owning his own vintage vehicle restoration company. He was a self-taught mechanic and besides figuring it out on his own, he learned all that he knew from watching his grandfather fix up his 1965 Ford F100. Which was passed down to him when his grandfather passed on to glory. He expressed his love for vintage cars and attending car shows was one of his favorite pastimes. His mother and father had been together his whole life and was still madly in love. He had a normal upbringing, but peer pressure started him on a bad path.

We sat there talking, eating and enjoying each other's company for hours. Time flew like an arrow through the wind and before we knew it, the sun joined us for breakfast.

School started in a few hours, and I was dreading the thought of being expected to function normally on an hour or two of sleep.

He noticed the tiredness of my eyes and I noticed the same in his. He paid for our tab, and we made our way back to the hellcat.

Chapter Five

"So, Gautier street it is, right?"

"Yes, that's right," I chirped.

"Since your mom put you out, are you going to live with this friend from now on? Like, what is the plan after tonight? I don't mean to get all in your business, I'm just curious."

"Honestly, Echo, I don't know. Tasia's mom works a lot so I will probably have a couple of nights before she notices that I'm there. After that, who knows. I'll figure something out. I'm damn sure not going back to my mama's house if that is what you are asking."

"Listen, I know that this is sudden and may sound crazy but why don't you come stay with me?"

I side-eyed him because there was no way that I was about to put myself under someone else's thumb.

"Before you start thinking the worse, it's not like that," he smiled. "I have my own crib, and you can come crash with me. It's a two bedroom and no one will bother you there. Not even me."

"Umm, that sounds nice, Echo, but you don't know me, and I don't know you like that. Are you really offering for me to come stay with you? Why would you do that?"

"Because I want to help. One question tho...Do you think that anyone will come looking for you? I mean yes, you are seventeen, but you are still considered a minor. I don't need the police sniffing around my shit."

"I don't think you have to worry about that," I shrugged. "If anything, they will be looking for your ass. You are the one robbing corner stores, remember." We both giggled.

"Echo, are you sure about this? Why do all of this for someone you just met a few hours ago? For all you know, I could get in your shit and rob you blind."

"Gigi, please. You are not about that life. I can tell," he said as he smiled and waved me off. "And yes I'm sure. It's nothing wrong with helping people from time to time. I see that you are trying to make the best out of a bad situation, and I want to look out. You seem real chill and I like that about you."

"I see. I guess I'm just not used to people helping me in any way without asking for something in return. You don't want anything from me, right? I don't have a lot of money. I can't help you pay rent or anything like that. I do plan on getting a job and I can help out then."

"Gigi, don't worry about any of that. My rent is paid up for the whole year, so I don't need your money. The only thing I want from you is to keep your grades up and keep your shit together. I messed up my opportunity by doing stupid shit and being careless, but I don't want you to mess up yours."

"Boy stop. You still have time to right your wrongs. I'll help you. If you say that you didn't do half bad, then I'm sure that taking that G.E.D will be a breeze. You just have to start believing in yourself and give yourself some grace." I said with a smile.

"I see you're young, but wise. That sounded like something my grandfather would say and I'm not being hard on myself...I'm taking accountability. I've fucked up in a lot of ways, but I'm learning from my mistakes. I'm moving a lot differently from the way I use to."

"Good, but seriously though, thank you for letting me stay with you. Nobody's ever done anything this nice for me, Echo. I honestly don't even know how to accept kindness that isn't attached to anything."

"Don't mention it. It's not a big deal."

I knew Tasia was expecting me, and I didn't want to be rude and just not show up, so I sent her a text message.

Me: Bitch, lock your door. I'm not coming but I will see you later on in school today. Thank you anyway though.

Tasia: Girl, WTF happened. You got me sitting up here waiting on your tail.

Me: I'll tell you later. TTYS

Tasia: Later boo

WE CRUISED for about fifteen additional minutes before pulling into a posh neighborhood that I had no idea existed in our little town. I mean, why would I? It's not like my mama ever took me anywhere this nice. We stopped at his gate, where he and the guard chopped it up. He introduced me, letting him know that I had full access to come and go. I smiled, waved goodbye and in just a few short seconds, we arrived in his driveway. I assumed that he had an apartment, but it was a townhouse. A nice one with a manicured lawn, a two-car garage and a beautiful lake in the backyard.

"Now wait a damn minute, Echo. I know you work at Jiffy Lube, but I know damn well they aren't paying you enough to live in a place like this. If they are, can you please bring me an application?" I said, admiring how nice it was.

He chuckled, "No Gigi. Jiffy Lube is not how I was able to afford this place. My grandpa is. When he died, he left me more than that truck. He left me a few acres of land and a nice little chunk of change. It's how I got the Hellcat and this place. The only thing is, that money is gone. Almost every cent of it. I was balling out of control like my name was Future until one day I looked up, and that account was damn near empty.

Take it from me, if you ever run into big money, get someone you can trust to help you manage it. I didn't, and I fucked up bad. I'm good now though. I've been saving and I'm back on track," he announced, grabbing my bags from the backseat.

Hitting the garage clicker, it opened, revealing the Ford truck that he spoke so highly of and a well-kept Nissan Maxima.

"Gigi, can you drive?"

"Yes, I can but I don't have my license. Why do you ask?"

"Because you see that Maxima right there? It's just been sitting there for months and I don't drive it. You can use it to get yourself back and forth to school. If I were you, I'd take the back roads, you know, since you're not legal yet." We walked past the cars, and he stopped to show me where the car keys were kept.

Once we got into the house, I was in awe. The place was decked out. A bachelor's pad for sure, but a very fancy one. Someone had to help him decorate this. There's no way someone this young had such great taste.

I scanned every corner of the room. I'd never seen anything so well put together before, and I couldn't believe that this would be my home. For a little while, at least.

We ascended the steps, and I discovered that the bedroom covered the entire second floor. Huge didn't begin to describe it. It was also decorated to the nines, just like downstairs. Boasting a gorgeous canopy bedroom set with intricate designs. It was modern looking yet traditional at the same time. The bed was adorned with a cute pink comforter set with big fluffy pillows and a fluffy rug to match. The bathroom had everything a girl could ever ask for: a huge garden bathtub and separate shower, a makeup vanity, and a walk-in closet so big that it was going to make my five little outfits look sickly in there all alone.

"Umm, Echo, I know that this is your place, but if I didn't know any better, I'd think that a woman already lived here. Please tell me that I'm wrong," I said, nervously staring at the pink curtains draped across the windows.

"Oh nah, it's not like that but you are half right. My little sister comes over and stays with me every now and then. That's my baby. She's only eleven but acts thirty. Hopefully, you'll get the chance to meet her. Listen, it's late, and I know that you are tired, so please make yourself at home. I'm gonna bring your things up here in a minute. Why don't you go ahead and lie down? It's almost 6 am, so at least you can get a little sleep before school." He attempted to touch my hand. Flinching, I pulled back without even meaning to.

"I didn't mean to scare you. I'm sorry, I shouldn't have done that," he said empathetically.

"It's cool, Echo. I didn't mean to flinch. It was just my reflexes. I'm not scared. You are good. I promise."

"I'm sorry once again." He nervously apologized and headed back down the stairs to get my things, then quietly left them at the door.

Chapter Six

I walked around the room, taking it all in. Sitting on the edge of the bed, I couldn't help but thank God for putting me in the right place at the right time. Who would have thought that walking in on a robbery would lead to this. I also thanked him for blessing Echo with a good heart. Good enough to offer a complete stranger a warm bed and a place safe from trauma and agony.

I sauntered into the bathroom to take a shower. My normal 15-minute shower quickly turned into a 45-minute shower as I scrubbed my body for the old and new. I attempted to scrub away 17 years of sorrow, hurt and pain. In my mind, I was scrubbing away all the shame, fear and depression. I was scrubbing away the old stench of all the men who enjoyed my body against my will. Scrubbing away the verbal abuse and insults that were hurled at me for all those years.

In that shower, I promised myself that I would never go back to that place again. As a matter of fact, I would never go to any place that resembled that place. This was a new beginning for me, but I knew that new beginnings sometimes started with forgiveness. I called out to God to help me with that. He and I both knew that my mother didn't deserve it, but it wasn't for her, it was for me. Undeserving and all, I forgave her so that I could move forward, and not be stuck in the past.

Getting out of the shower, I felt lighter than I had in years. I decided that it wasn't even worth it to go to sleep. The couple of hours I'd get wouldn't have done anything but piss me off. Instead, I got dressed and made my way back downstairs to find Echo asleep on the couch.

Grabbing the blanket from the arm of the sofa, I covered him, then sat in the recliner next to him. I found myself staring at him adoringly, counting the freckles across his nose. I didn't want to look at him like a savior because I knew that there was only one, but I was so appreciative of him and his kindness. After what I'd been through, I thought that I'd always have a strong hatred for all men. It is surprising how one act of kindness can help soften the hardest of hearts.

After a while, I lightly pushed his shoulder, waking

him. "Echo, hey love, I hate to bother you because you were sleeping so peacefully, but I wanted to let you know that I'm leaving for school. Will you be here when I get back, or do you have to work today?"

"No, Lil Thugger, no work today, so I'll be here chilling. Ummm, wait," he said as he dug in his pockets. "Here's fifty dollars. Make sure you stop by the gas station and fill up so you'll be good for the rest of the week. I'm going grocery shopping today so we'll have something to eat in this bitch. I usually go over to my folk's house to eat, but maybe we can have dinner here a couple of nights a week. Can you cook? Cause I can't even boil water."

"Yes, I can cook. My mama damn sure couldn't, so I had to. I can burn with the best of them. My granny taught me," I bragged.

"Okay then, have a good day and be safe out there. I'll see you when you get home."

Home. He really just said...see you when you get *home*. I can't believe this shit.

Hopping in the car, I adjusted the seats and mirrors. Damn, he's tall. Does Shaq drive this damn car? I turned the ignition and she purred like a kitten. Putting her in reverse and backing out of the garage proved to be a bit difficult for me. It had been ages since I'd been behind the wheel of a car, but I managed. I pulled out successfully and was off. I waved at the guard at the gate and hit the highway.

While driving, I realized I was going to have to work diligently to retrain my brain to think positively. The minute he put the money in my hand, my first instinct was to stuff it under the mattress, afraid my mother would find it and use it for drugs. I no longer had to do that, and it felt too good. I stopped at the gas station, filled up, and even had enough change to grab a quick breakfast before school.

I hit the high school parking lot feeling like that bitch. The truth was, I didn't have a pot to piss in or a window to throw it out of. However, I was old enough to know that when you know better, you do better, and I was hell-bent on doing just that. I breezed through the day, and although I was exhausted, I managed to ace my test. I didn't miss a beat.

Tasia had been on my heels all day, wanting to know more about last night. Not having the energy to gossip, I told her I would call her after I got home and got some sleep.

Once my classes were done, I made a beeline back to the house, arriving to find Echo's car gone. Letting myself in, I ran to my bedroom. I was too tired to get comfortable, so I didn't even attempt to change clothes. I slid under the covers and slept like a newborn baby.

I woke up what felt like minutes later, but had to be hours. It was pitch-black outside. The house was so quiet it made me nervous. I was so used to functioning in chaos that calm felt suspicious. I made a mental note to work on that too.

Rolling out of bed, I noticed a pair of fuzzy house shoes on the floor. I didn't recall seeing them when I fell asleep, or maybe I had, but I'd been too tired to notice. Reaching to turn on the lamp, I saw a pajama set at the bottom of my bed. I hated to assume anything, but in this case, I had to assume these things were for me.

I entered the bathroom and started the shower when I saw a sink full of hair products, facial products, and feminine items. From the corner of my eye, I spotted brand new clothes hanging in the closet. I skipped over to the closet to make sure I wasn't tripping. My eyes weren't playing tricks on me. I had a whole new wardrobe. There were brand new jeans, tops, dresses, shoes, and even accessories. Overwhelmed with gratitude, I turned off the shower and ran downstairs to find Echo. He was in the kitchen putting away groceries when I ran and jumped in his arms.

Chapter Seven

"Thank you so much for everything. All the things you got me...the clothes, the pajamas, shit..just all of it. I needed them so badly, but I was just going to make do with what I had. I appreciate it more than you'll ever know."

"You're welcome. I had my mom go shopping with me today. I told her I had a new girlfriend and wanted to get her some nice things, and she did her thing. Did you see the stuff I got for you in the dresser? I got you new bras, underwear, and socks... the whole nine. I hope they're the right size. I don't know shit about bras."

"Yes, I saw it all." Before I could finish my statement, he added,"Gigi, I know you're tough. I would imagine you're going to tell me you don't want any handouts but damn all that. Like I told you earlier, I just wanted to help, so I did."

"Echo, normally I would talk shit, but for the first time in a long time, I'm at a loss for words. I love everything in that closet. I can't even front, and I'd be lying to you if I said I didn't need them because I do. I've had this same shit for years now. My titties and ass have grown since then, so all of it was too small. So yes, a whole new wardrobe was needed. I was just going to thug it out, like I always do. So thank you for thinking of me. Also, please thank your mom for having the taste that she does. Now I see why this place is so laid. There's a woman's touch all over this house."

"Yes, Mom Dukes is the shit. My biggest supporter. That lady loves me through thick and thin, and I love her right back."

"Now, don't think I didn't notice that you told your mom you had a new girlfriend."

"Gigi, don't trip on that statement. I didn't want to put your business out there. I told her that so she wouldn't ask me a thousand questions. Nothing more, nothing less."

"Good, because I'm trying to focus on getting my shit together. Graduating high school and doing something with my life is the ultimate goal. All that other shit can come later. You and I both are so young. We have our whole lives ahead of us, and plenty of time for that."

With all I'd been through, a relationship was the last thing I wanted.

"You're right, Thugger," he laughed. "So, what can you cook? I bought all kinds of shit. Come take a look."

As he opened the fridge, I almost drooled a little. It looked like he bought the whole grocery store. The first thing that caught my eye were the fresh vegetables and fruit. Something I hadn't had in ages. My mama always got groceries that were going bad to save money. Nothing she brought home was ever fresh.

Then I noticed the meat. It was so pretty I would have sworn he butchered it himself. There were ribeyes, T-bone steaks, ground beef, turkey, and chicken. He even bought lamb and seafood, two things that I loved, but we never could afford. The freezer was full as well. I grabbed the ground beef, one egg, one onion, bell pepper, a few potatoes, heavy cream, and the fresh green beans.

I proceeded to cook the best meatloaf, mashed potatoes, and green beans I'd ever made in my life. He watched TV as I prepared a meal fit for a king. Once everything was done, I fixed his plate, took it to him, and we sat in the living room and enjoyed our dinner. I put every ounce of joy, happiness, and love I had into preparing the food, and the taste reflected it. I figured

Echo deserved a good home-cooked meal, especially for what he'd done for me.

"Damn, Gigi, you didn't lie, girl. You sure know how to throw down in the kitchen. I could get used to some shit like this."

"I'm gonna have to teach you how to cook, Echo. You need to at least learn the basics so you won't have to rely on anyone else to put food in your belly."

He shot me a look, and I bucked my eyes back at him.

"For now, you don't have to worry about that because I'll handle all the cooking. You can look forward to meals like this often."

"Since you cooked, I guess I should get my ass up and wash these dishes. That's how my mom and dad used to do it, so it only seems right," he said.

"I'm gonna go hop in the shower while you do that, then I'll put on those cozy PJs and those comfy house shoes you bought me. I'll be right back down." I grinned as big as Texas. "You want to watch a movie or something when I come back?"

"Yeah, we can do that. Hurry up though. Your ass slept half the day away."

"Now that wasn't my fault. It was only supposed to be a little nap. My body said, 'Bitch, lay your ass down,' and I had no choice but to comply. I'm taking my ass to bed tonight, so you don't have to worry about that."

I ran back upstairs, started my shower again, and jumped in. I couldn't stop the corners of my mouth from going upward. My jaws hurt because I was grinning so much. If this is what happiness felt like, sign me up for a lifetime supply of this shit.

Living in a state of depression and misery had been my norm for as long as I could remember. No child should ever have to endure the things I did, and that thought alone started the tears flowing.

I had to be strong for so long that I couldn't even remember the last time I cried. Releasing the hurt felt so good.

My mama always told me that crying was for weak bitches, but I felt more powerful than ever before. I knew that at some point, I was going to have to face the demon I call Mama, but I'd rather do it when I'm in a better place mentally. Dealing with her now, so soon after forgiving her, might bring out a side of me that I was desperately trying to bury.

Chapter Eight

The next couple of weeks went off without a hitch. Echo and I lived together and got along famously. I attended school every day, excelling in all my classes, while he went to work. By the time he arrived home, dinner was cooked, and the house was clean. I'd even drawn him a bath a time or two. We either watched a little TV together or ended up asleep on the couch after dinner.

On the weekends, he always found something for us to do. Whether it be visiting an aquarium, track racing, attending car shows or just a simple picnic in the park. We were always together.

He was the first man I'd ever spent this much time with who didn't want anything from me. Well, except the occasional back rub, but even that was innocent.

This had become our routine, and it seemed to be working for both of us. He appeared to be thriving, and so was I.

Then one day his mother dropped by. She and I had a long conversation. She told me she had noticed positive changes in her son and was extremely grateful that I'd come into his life when I did.

She noted that he seemed more responsible and self-aware than ever before and hinted that I was the reason that he'd finally started showing the greatness she always knew he possessed.

I wanted to tell her that it was actually the other way around but doing that would've meant talking about my past, and I wasn't ready for that.

She didn't know me, but she thought the world of me. My truth might've changed that, so I stayed tight-lipped.

She was very long-winded and loved to talk, so I let her. I sat there and listened.

"His father and I were so concerned about his future. Echo was hanging out with the wrong crowd and made some bad decisions in the past. He was putting his trust in the wrong people. They had my baby stealing cars, smoking weed and he even called himself selling drugs at one time.

My husband and I had to step in a few times to get him out of trouble, but since you've been around, he's been on the straight and narrow. We raised him to do the right thing and be a good person and my baby seems to be doing just that. I'm so proud of his growth. This is the happiest I've seen Echo in years."

Then she started prying, asking where I came from, what my parents' names were. The typical questions a parent asks someone their child is dating. Of course, I deflected without a second thought. The way I was raised, I'd mastered the art of dodging questions.

After our conversation ended, she hugged me, kissed me on the cheek, and bid me adieu. Once I shut the door behind her, I pulled up a seat at the dining room table. I should've felt uplifted, but instead, I felt guilty.

On one hand, I agreed with her to an extent. Echo really did seem to be in a great headspace. But I hated that she thought it was because of me.

Her son had done more for me than anyone else in my life. Besides my granny of course, and I thanked God every day for our chance encounter. On the other hand, I often felt like a burden to him. He was literally taking care of me, handling all my needs and even some of my wants. I never wanted to rely on a man for anything. And yet, here I was... relying on him for everything.

He never complained about me being here, but he didn't have to. My conscience ate away at me daily. I told my mother I would never be like her, but here I was, a full-on dependent. He might as well had claimed me on his taxes.

But I had a plan to fix that. I was set to graduate in a couple of months, in May. And with my birthday at the end of April, I'd finally be able to join the Armed Forces. My school hosted a career day, and the military recruiters spoke to us about all the opportunities they could offer. I made an appointment to take the ASVAB two days after my eighteenth birthday.

I wanted to take it earlier, but that would've required parental consent. That wasn't an option, so I had no choice but to wait. Prayerfully, I'd do well. Then I could let Echo know I'd be out of his hair for good. He could finally have his bachelor pad back. Until then, we'd continue living our lives as normal. And I would quietly count down the days until I could leave everything...including Roseville, Alabama behind.

Chapter Nine

Echo came home in a great mood, alluding that he had a surprise for me and to meet him out back by the lake. I threw on the Crocs he bought me and ran out back to find a little Maltipoo running around. It had to be the cutest thing I'd ever seen. I absolutely loved animals and always wanted one, but of course, I was never able to keep any pets. My mother would sell practically anything we had to support her habit.

The puppy ran and jumped into my arms, and my heart almost burst with joy.

"Echo!" I screamed. "Is it a girl or boy?"

"Turn her over. Do you see any balls back there? I don't think you do, so it's a girl," he laughed.

She was so lovable and fluffy. I picked her up and

hugged her like I gave birth to her. I had a feeling she'd become a great friend to me.

"Gigi, I was so scared when I got her because we've never talked about having animals before. I didn't know how you'd feel about me bringing home a furry roommate. Especially without knowing if you were allergic or scared of dogs. But she was so cute that I couldn't pass her up. Plus, she was free-ninety-nine."

"Wait...you mean to tell me you got this expensive-ass dog for free? How?"

"There was a couple giving dogs away at the Walmart in town. They said they couldn't afford to keep the litter. Their only condition was making sure they went to a good home. She's the one that kept staring at me, and when I picked her up, she licked my face.

I couldn't just leave her. So, I got her. Now come on and put some clothes on. Let's go to the pet shop and find her some toys, a dog bed, and shit like that."

"Shit, Echo, give me about ten minutes and I'll be ready. I was just getting ready to start dinner, so let me go back in here and put this food away. Maybe we can do takeout tonight. My treat," I said as I trekked back up to the townhouse.

"Hurry up. Oh, and Gigi, you've got to name her. What are you going to call her?"

"I don't know, love. I'll come up with something, I'm

sure," I yelled as I entered the back door. As I rushed upstairs to change, my phone rang, it was Tasia.

"Girl, what do you want? You can't miss me that bad. I just saw your ass at school."

"Well damn, bitch. Hello to you too. I got my mama's car for the evening, and I was wondering if you wanted some company. Can I come by and chill with you for a bit?"

"Let me go ask Echo if he feels like having people over. You know this isn't my spot, so I can't just be inviting folks without asking. That's rude. My granny did teach me some manners. I'll call you back after I see what he says."

"I'm not just folks though, I'm your bestie. But okay then. Go ask your man and call me back."

"I thought I told you a thousand times already that he is not my man. He's my friend. Now bye, with your messy ass," I chirped, hanging up the phone.

I finished getting dressed and ran back downstairs. He and the puppy were sitting on the couch, and they both were so stinking cute.

"Come on, Echo and little puppy...let's go. I'm so excited!" I screamed.

"Girl, calm your ass down," he laughed.

"I can't help it! I've never had a puppy of my own before. Look at me, already claiming her. She's ours, but I just know she's going to love me more than she loves you,"

I teased. "I'm officially a dog mama!" I cackled, dancing in the garage.

"Honestly, I got her for you, so you have every right to call her your dog. Now, Ms. Mamas, what are you going to name her?" He asked as we hopped into the car and backed out of the driveway.

"I think I'll call her Sheba. Do you like that? It has a nice ring to it, doesn't it?"

"Yes, it does. Sheba works for me."

"Echo, are you sure you want to go to the pet store? You must be trying to spend big money. We can get all of the things she needs for way cheaper. You better drive this damn car up to Walmart. We can get her bed, food, and everything else there."

He took my advice, and we pulled up to Wally World. Sheba was so small that she fit in my purse. As I snuggled her in, he came around and opened my door. We headed into the store where he grabbed a buggy. While strolling to the pet section, I saw my mother out the corner of my eye and ducked into the clothing section as fast as I could.

I was in a good headspace, and I refused to let her mess it up. I also didn't want Echo to meet her, because then I'd feel compelled to give him more of my past than I was ready to.

. . .

"GIRL, WHAT ARE YOU DOING?" he asked. "I thought we were going to the pet section. Why are you over here hiding in the clothes?"

"Because I saw someone over there that I don't want to talk to or see me. Let me stay here until she leaves. You go on ahead and I'll meet you over there in a few minutes," I said as I shooed him away.

"You sure, Gigi?"

"Yes, I'm sure. Positive," I yelled. "Please, just go."

He did, and I instantly felt like stir-fried shit for yelling at him like that. He was only trying to understand what was happening. I stood there and watched my mother until she checked out or stole whatever she had. Finally, she left the store, and I breathed a sigh of relief as I jogged back to the pet section. There he stood with a bewildered look on his face.

"Before you say anything, let me apologize for yelling. I didn't mean to react like that. I'm sorry. My mom was up there, and I didn't want to deal with her."

He looked up at the ceiling and rolled his eyes before he voiced, "Whatever you say, Gigi. You act really strange whenever someone brings up your mother or your family. You've met my mom...she told me she stopped by and talked with you. Yet, I still don't know a single thing about you besides the fact that your mother put you out.

I'm not going to try to force you to talk about her,

because it's obviously deeper than what you've said. But I want you to know that no matter what you tell me; I won't judge you.

I know you're a good person. So, whatever your past is...it's just that, your past. But it does kind of bother me a little that you won't give me any of you. Like I said I'm not trying to force you, but I do want you to know how I feel."

Inhaling sharply, I muttered, "I'm sorry for closing you out, Echo. I don't talk about my family because it's so much to unpack. I've dealt with all kinds of trauma, and I'm not yet comfortable talking about it. Maybe one day I'll sit you down and tell you everything, but that won't be today. Now, can we go ahead and get Sheba the things she needs? She's starting to get antsy in this bag."

Chapter Ten

Echo and I strolled the pet aisle to figure out what to purchase for my new baby. I grabbed all the necessities like dog food, shampoo, a crate, puppy pads, treats, a cute little leash and collar, squeaky toys, and soft, comfortable bedding.

"Damn, Gigi, just buy out the whole store while you're at it," he giggled.

"Oh, Echo, I got so caught up with Sheba that I forgot to ask if it was okay to have company. My friend Tasia wants to come over. Since it's your house, I told her I'd ask you first."

Grabbing my hand, he said, "You know you hurt my feelings when you say stuff like that, right? It's your house too. I wish you'd stop looking at it like you're a visitor. Don't you realize by now that I actually like having you there? If I didn't, you wouldn't be. It's that simple. And I'm not your father, so you don't have to ask permission to do anything. If you want to have a friend over, that's fine with me. If I don't want to be bothered, I'll go to my room and close the door."

"Echo, I feel like I'm always doing or saying something to hurt your feelings. It makes me sad because that's not at all what I want to do. I need you to understand that I'm not used to being in a healthy environment. That's one of the reasons why I don't say much. My people and communication skills are shit, but I'm working on that. Please just give me time. I love the friendship we have. I don't want to damage or tarnish it in any way. That's why I tread so lightly. I just don't want to fuck this up," I confessed, as we walked up to the checkout counter.

Shaking his head, he pulled out his debit card. I stopped him.

"No, Echo, I've got this," I proudly muttered.

"You sure? I got her for you, so I fully expected to cover the cost."

"And that's exactly why I don't want you to. You take care of everything. Please, let me get this. I know I don't have a lot of money, but if she's going to be my dog, then I need to contribute to her care in some way," I insisted.

I pulled out my wallet and paid for all of Sheba's things

before heading back to the Hellcat. He popped the trunk and loaded the goodies as I hopped into the front seat.

He returned the buggy, flopped down beside me, and just stared. It made me a little uncomfortable because I didn't know what this was about. I was nervous, but I tried to keep my poker face on.

After a few moments, he turned to me and said, "You know, you said something back there that makes me wonder. You said you don't want to fuck this up, and I'm sitting here trying to figure out why you would even think like that. Have I said or done anything to make you feel like you're fucking this up? The answer is no." he griped.

"I know I said I wouldn't force you to tell me anything, but you've got to give me something, because you're right. The way you think is extremely unhealthy. I've done my best to show you nothing but love and not in a freaky way either, but in a genuine, 'I give a damn' kind of way. Yet you don't know how to receive it. I'm young, but I'm old enough to know something's not right. Don't get me wrong...I'm not trying to insult or upset you but there's something I'm missing."

"Can we not talk about this, please? Can we just go get Chinese food and go home?"

"No, we can't. You never want to have hard conversations. Just because they're hard doesn't mean they aren't needed."

"Echo, please. Not now."

"Gigi, communication is important in any relationship. Friendship or otherwise. Why don't you just talk to me? I don't bite and I won't hurt you. Don't you understand that by now? You are one of the best things that's ever happened to me. I wouldn't jeopardize that. I would do anything to see you smile."

His words touched my heart like nothing had before. I wanted to tell him the truth, but I just couldn't. This wasn't the right time. I tried to fight back my tears, but I lost. As soon as one tear fell from my eye, Echo went into panic mode.

"Oh my God, Gigi, I'm so sorry. I didn't mean to make you cry. You don't have to talk about anything you don't want to. I overstepped, and I'll never do that again."

He grabbed a tissue from his console and gently wiped the tears from my eyes.

"Please just forget that this conversation ever happened. Go ahead and call your friend back and tell her to come over. We'll eat, play with Sheba, and play cards or something," he said nervously.

"Echo, I'm not crying because you hurt my feelings. I'm crying because I've never had anyone show the love and care that you have. That is what's overwhelming...not you wanting to talk about the hard things. That's expected. What I didn't expect was your gentleness and concern."

"Everybody deserves common decency, Gigi. I honestly don't understand what I'm doing that's so special."

"The way you treat me is special. You're so considerate and attentive. That is where the tears are coming from. But thank you for letting it go. I promise you that when the time is right, I'll tell you everything."

Chapter Eleven

Leaving the Walmart parking lot, we made our way to our local Chinese food spot to order takeout. Once we got our food, we hit the highway heading home. I looked over at Echo; he was quiet and looked to be deep in thought. I made the phone call to Tasia to give her the address and told her to come on over.

We rode the rest of the way home in silence. Once in the garage, he killed the motor and apologized once again. I reassured him that everything was okay, and he gave me the most heartfelt hug. He melted in my arms, and surprisingly, I did the same. I immediately took Sheba to the grass to let her potty. By the time she decided to go, Tasia was pulling up.

Echo retrieved the bags out of the trunk and entered the house while I stayed outside with Sheba.

Tasia slid out of her car, already with the bullshit.

"Girl, you did not tell me that he lived in this nice-ass neighborhood. This is definitely a step up from where you came from."

"What the fuck is that supposed to mean? Are you trying to be funny, bitch?" I said in a serious tone.

"Not at all. I'm just observing my surroundings. No wonder why you don't mess with me anymore. You're over here living the good life, and you've got a good nigga taking care of you. You just forgot about little old me."

"We are not about to do this again, Tasia. Just bring your ass on in the house. We ordered takeout, and I got you your favorite, sesame chicken."

"Thank you, Frennn! You know I love me some sesame chicken," she said as she followed me through the garage door.

By now, Echo had taken his normal seat on the couch and was watching television. He'd already fixed his plate but hadn't touched it.

"Echo, why aren't you eating?"

"Because you were outside. I was waiting for you to come back in so we could eat together, like we always do."

"But you say that ain't your nigga," Tasia whispered under her breath.

"Shut up, Tasia. Damn, you are so messy."

"Okay, give me a minute to wash my hands and fix my plate, and then we can all eat."

"All you have to do is wash your hands. I've already fixed your plate, and it's in the microwave. Tasia, I put your takeout bowl on the stove and a plate beside it. I'll let you make your own plate because I don't know your preferences. I hope that's cool."

"So, he made your plate but didn't make mine? Sounds like your man to me, Sis."

"Tasia, I swear, if you say another motherfucking word, I will put you the fuck out." I said, looking her in the eyes to let her know I wasn't fucking around.

I washed my hands, grabbed my plate, and took my normal seat beside Echo. Tasia fixed her plate and sat on the couch opposite Echo and me.

Her ass barely touched the cushions before she started with the questions.

"So, Echo, how long have you lived in this neighborhood?"

"I've been here for almost a year now."

"Oh, okay. I've got to compliment you on your home. It is beautiful. Gigi, I bet that staying in a place like this took some getting used to. Especially in comparison to that shit hole you grew up in."

I sucked my teeth and griped, "Tasia, if you're talking to him, then talk to him. There's no need for you to slide that slick shit about me into the conversation. You're starting to piss me off."

Echo looked at me a bit confused and replied, "Thank you. I have my mom to thank for that. She came and did the decorating for me."

"Well, let me tell you, your mother has great taste. She did her thing. Soooooo, are you originally from Roseville because you are fine as hell and you've got a face that I think I'd remember. I've never seen you before."

I cut my eyes at her as Echo began to answer her question, because what type of shit was she on tonight?

He looked at me before answering. "Thank you for the compliment. Anyway, I wasn't born here, but my father was. I've been here most of my life though. We moved here when I was about five. My father was in the military and we traveled a lot. He was medically retired, and we ended up settling back here. I went to a private school in the next county, so that's probably why you've never seen me around."

"Oh, is that so?" Tasia remarked, acting like she really gave a damn, when she was really just being nosy.

"I like that Hellcat you whip. How in the hell can you afford a Hellcat? Do you work, or are you a dope boy? I'm just asking because Gigi refuses to tell me anything about y'all's relationship, but it looks like you two are doing good as hell. Shit, I wanna be like y'all when I grow up."

"Okay, Tasia, damn. That's enough with the questions. How about you eat your food and hush? He can't even chew and swallow before you throw out another question. He isn't on trial."

"Well, damn, Gigi, just eat me up then. All I'm trying to do is see and get to know the man that has taken my best friend from me."

"He hasn't taken shit. You're right here with me, aren't you? All I did was move. That's it. And being that you know what I was moving away from, I would think that you would be happy for me. You're supposed to be my friend, right? Because you sure as fuck aren't acting like it right now," I spat.

Smiling, Tasia let out, "Let's be for real. You've done more than move, but I'm happy for you. At least you don't have to run for your life in the middle of the night anymore or catch a cab to my house to get away from all those niggas. I'm glad you don't have to do the shit you used to do."

"Tasia, please!!! Just stop. Are you trying to fuck up my night? Nobody asked you any of that shit."

"So, he doesn't know?"

I cut my eyes at her, telling her to shut the fuck up without parting my lips, but she didn't stop.

"Has he met Mama yet?" Tasia asked. "Echo, you need to meet Mama Shanice. She is a real trip. I can't tell you how many times that lady passed out on us. High off those damn pills. One time, she even tried to get me to give one of her---."

Chapter Twelve

"Okay, Tasia, I think it's time for you to go before I spazz out on your ass," I said, cutting her off mid-sentence.

"What do you mean go? I just got here. I didn't even finish my food."

"Who's damn fault is that? If you would have been chewing instead of running your muthafucking mouth, you'd be done by now. It's already in a to-go container, so you can take it with you. Grab your shit and bounce."

She got up, grabbed her sweater and her doggie bag, and I showed her to the door.

"Bye, Girl," she said with a slick-ass grin on her face.

I started to slap the fire from her ass, but instead, I just pushed her out and slammed the door behind her.

"Gigi, what was that about? That's a weird-ass friendship you and her have."

"Fuck her, Echo. She's always had a hater spirit, and tonight it reared its ugly head. If I ever doubted whether she fucked with me the long way, tonight proved to me she damn sure doesn't. I don't want or need people like that around me. I have enough shit to deal with. The last thing I need is a no-good ass bitch talking about things that don't even matter anymore."

"You're right. It doesn't matter anymore, so why would you let her get you that upset?"

"Because I'm trying to leave my past where it is, and she sits in my face, trying to little girl me. I don't appreciate that shit at all. She's mad because she feels like I don't deal with her like I used to, and it's true. I don't, but now you see why."

"I feel you. If one of my boys tried to handle me like that, I'd probably crash out on their ass too."

"The worst thing you can have is an enemy disguised as a friend," I quipped. "OOOhhh, Echo, I'm so damn mad. I don't even have an appetite anymore. I am super pissed."

"Gigi, calm down. There's no need for all that. Give her the benefit of the doubt. Maybe she was really just trying to get to know me."

"No, Echo, what she wanted to do was be the messy bitch that she is. You know, I've seen her do other girls like that, but I never thought she'd do it to me. She really tried it. I should've mashed her head into the fucking wall and made Sheba bite her damn ankles."

Echo cracked up laughing. "Seriously, Gigi. Calm down. Everything is okay. That *was* kind of crazy because I thought she was your homegirl."

"Me too. It took me till right now to realize that Tasia is the type of bitch that wants to see you doing good but not better than her. I can't relate. When I say I'm happy for people, I truly mean it. One thing about me, I am a loyal friend, and I don't have an envious bone in my body, unlike that condescending ass bitch."

"Gigi, you have to understand that everyone isn't going to have the same heart as you, and that's okay. I want you to calm down and relax. It's been a long day."

"It sure has," I concurred.

"So, why don't you go upstairs and take a hot bath? I'll take Sheba out for a walk and make sure she goes potty, as you call it, and then put her up for the night. Then you can go to bed. Hopefully, you'll have a better day tomorrow."

"Today was a good day, especially with you bringing Sheba home. If it weren't for Tasia, I'd be good."

"What about you seeing your mother...that had you feeling a way also?"

"I know what to expect out of my mother. I didn't

expect that from Tasia. Anyhow, I'm going to take your advice and get in the tub and soak for a little while. Once again, thank you for everything, and I'll see you in the morning." I slid my arms under his and hugged him. As I tried to pull away, he hugged me tighter. He stood there and held me in his arms for what seemed like forever.

The longer we embraced, the more my anger faded. Embracing others was usually cringy for me, but with him, it was different. He had become my safe place. I never thought I'd be able to say that and truly believe it, but day after day, he exceeded my expectations. He made me want to love someone someday.

That wouldn't be possible anytime soon because I needed to get myself together and deal with my issues, but damn, he felt so good to me.

I pulled away, ran to my bedroom, and closed the door. He left me almost breathless. Realizing now that the wall I had meticulously built was coming down brick by brick, and if I'm honest with myself, I didn't like it. I put that wall there for a reason. I had a goal in mind, and I didn't want anything to deter me from reaching it. Not even love.

Chapter Thirteen

Autopilot had been my first and last name for the past few weeks. I'd developed a strict routine. After all, I was going to have one once I entered the military, so I figured I might as well start now and enact my own. I looked at it as a head start to greatness.

Sheba and I woke up every morning, and I'd take her outside to handle her business. Then I'd make a nice breakfast for Echo and me before heading off to school. After school, I'd come home and cook dinner. Then I'd take Sheba for a long walk in the evening. This had become my escape. It was a way to keep me out of my feelings...which I seemed to be in a lot. I realized I was becoming more and more attached to Echo, and this routine helped me create a little distance.

This became my norm, day in and day out, and before I knew it, my birthday was here. Growing up in my mama's house, my birthday was essentially unacknowledged, so there was no need to start making it a big deal now. I'd survived just fine without it being celebrated.

My eighteenth trip around the sun landed on a Saturday that year. I'd decided I would spend the day alone, reflecting on the last few months of my life and the positive changes I'd made. Echo didn't know it was my birthday, and I had no plans to tell him.

Hopping out of bed, I headed downstairs to get Sheba's day started. She was laying in her crate, eagerly waiting for me to free her. As soon as she saw me, she did her little dance of joy.

I grabbed her leash and led her out back to the lake to give her some freedom. This was her space. Where she could run, play, and just be herself. She went hard, as she should. She didn't have a care in the world. She didn't have to worry about what she'd eat or where she'd sleep. Someone else had already figured that out for her. Her only job was to be lovable, and she owned that role. In a way, I related to her. Echo had taken care of all my needs too...food, shelter, clothes. Maybe this was his thing, saving strays who needed someone to care.

While I was lost in thought, one of my favorite songs blasted through my headphones, and I did a little danceydance. I was jigging by the lake, without a care in the world, just like Sheba. I felt good. Blessed.

My mother never introduced me to God, but my grandmother talked about Him like they were best friends. She taught me to do the same. My faith was strong because of her. There were times I questioned God's presence in my life, but those times never lasted long. He always showed up for me, usually through someone else.

As I danced, I spoke to the Most High and thanked Him for another year. I thanked Him for giving me discernment, a sound mind, and a heart of gold that helped me survive. I was grateful for everything and counted my many blessings. Including Echo.

I was so into my moment with God, that I didn't notice Echo calling me from the back door. It wasn't until Sheba bolted toward him that I realized he was there. He waved and motioned for me to come inside.

"I didn't mean to interrupt your jigging," he said with a smile as I approached. "But I've got something I want to discuss with you."

Once inside, he asked me to sit down, and I couldn't help but wonder if I'd done something wrong. I was sure he'd noticed the emotional distance I'd been putting between us, and I hoped this wasn't about that.

"Gigi, I want to take you out tonight. You've been cooking two meals a day for a while now, and I want to do something nice for you. Let's go to a nice steakhouse. We can't drink, but we can have some mocktails," he said, chuckling. "Isn't that what you girls call them? Mocktails, right?"

I smiled. "Yes, they're called mocktails. What time are you thinking?"

"I want you to be ready by six. I have to stop by Ma Dukes' house before we head out. Apparently, I had a package delivered there, and I need to pick it up. That cool with you?"

"Hell yes! I love getting dressed and feeling pretty. It's not like I get to do it often. This gives me a chance to wear that fancy makeup you and your mom got me. Eeeekk!" I squealed with excitement.

"Good. I'm glad you're excited. And just so you know, you always look pretty to me. Now go check your bed. I bought you a dress for tonight. Try it on and see how it fits. You're a size 8, right?"

"Yep!" I chirped and dashed upstairs.

Laid out on the bed was the most beautiful dress I'd ever seen and in my favorite color, pink.

This man. He was so good to me. I didn't know what I'd done to deserve someone like him. If this was how he treated me as a friend, I could only imagine what it would be like to be his girl. I shook the thought off and focused on what I came upstairs to do.

As I started to undress, my fingers grazed the stretch marks on my hips. The tiger stripes on my thighs. The cigarette burns. The old belt and extension cord scars. The faded wound at my hairline, courtesy of a porcelain ashtray my mother once threw at me. I'd been through hell. But in a way, I was grateful. It made me tougher. It made me appreciate kindness, especially when it came without strings. It made me strong. My feelings were hard to hurt, but it was easy to piss me off.

Chapter Fourteen

Echo knocked on the door. "Let me see what it looks like," he called out, cracking the door a little to peek inside.

"I can't show you yet. I haven't even put it on. Besides, I don't want you to see me until we're ready to leave. Don't ruin this for me," I teased. "Let me be cute in peace."

"Okay, okay," he said. "But when you're done, come back down. I've got something else for you."

Damn. He may not have known it was my birthday, but he was treating me like royalty.

"Okay!" I shouted. "I'll be down in a few. Just gotta shower and brush my teeth."

"You hungry, Gigi?"

“Yes, but why do you ask? You know your ass can’t cook. Are you about to pick something up?”

He shot back playfully, “I just asked if you were hungry. Let me handle the rest.”

I was going to take a quick shower but changed my mind and decided to soak in the tub instead. I needed to enjoy the luxury of a real bath while I still could. There wouldn’t be any in basic training. Just two-minute showers, from what I’d heard.

But even in the tub, my mind refused to be still. I couldn’t relax, not really. My thoughts wouldn’t quiet themselves for shit... except during Echo’s embrace. That was the only time I felt fully at peace.

I closed my eyes and pictured six-year-old me, running around playing with a headless Barbie doll. One of my mother’s tricks thought it made a great birthday present. I remember being fussed at and called ungrateful for asking where the rest of the doll was.

That’s been my life. People giving me scraps and expecting me to be happy with it. But not anymore.

That little girl was gone. I was going to be that bitch and one day, they’d have no choice but to recognize it.

Since I couldn’t fully enjoy my bath like I wanted to, I got out, dried off, and threw on some comfy shorts and a camisole. It was still early, so I sauntered downstairs to see what Echo was up to.

The smell of bacon and French toast filled the air. Echo was in the kitchen, concentrating hard as hell, and I couldn't do anything but laugh.

I walked over to help him, but he stopped me in my tracks.

"Don't bring your ass over here, Gigi. I don't need any help. I've got this. Go sit on the end of the couch for me."

Doing as I was told; I sashayed to the couch and took a seat. Shortly after, he brought over a folding tray and set it in front of me. Then he headed back to the kitchen and returned with a plate featuring French toast, bacon, sausage, eggs, sliced strawberries, orange juice, and a single rose in a small flower vase.

"Awwww, this is so sweet. Thank you, Echo. You know you didn't have to do this. Why today? First the dress, now breakfast and dinner later. What's all this about?"

"Why do I need a reason to do something nice for you? Just showing you a lil' love. You know, Gigi, there are still some genuinely good people in this world, and I do my best to be one of them. Also, you should expect to be treated well. You deserve it. All women do. So please stop asking me why. *Because I wanted to*, is why."

He leaned over and kissed me on the forehead, and I wanted to disappear into the couch.

I had to admit, because of the sexual abuse I'd endured, touching, kissing, sex, or any version of intimacy intimidated me. That night I left my mother's house, I swore off men and declared that God himself would have to tap me on the shoulder, point at the man, and say, this is the one, in order for me to budge. And I swear, I felt God tapping me all the time about Echo, but I ignored it every time.

Because really. What were the chances that he was my person? Was he really the one God made for me? Would God really give me my soulmate this early? If so, why? Why would He give me someone so amazing when He knew I was ill-equipped to love him the way he deserved? These were the questions that ran through my mind, but I could never bring myself to question God. I was too afraid of the answers.

Once again, I shook off my thoughts and marveled at the delicious-looking food Echo had prepared. He brought his own tray, sat beside me, grabbed my hand, and said grace. We both dug in. Sheba was over in the corner enjoying her food too.

"I don't know how you miraculously learned to cook, but this is delicious. This French toast is bussin', Echo. Thank you again. It felt good to sleep in and have a nice meal made for me."

"You're welcome. And... YouTube."

"Excuse me? YouTube?" I repeated.

"Yes, you asked me where I learned to cook. I'm telling

you that it was YouTube. I watched about ten videos and decided last night that I was going to get up and fix breakfast for us. You always cook for me, so it was time I returned the favor."

"Well, let me thank YouTube because you sure as hell put your foot in it. This isn't regular French toast. This is some fancy shit," I chuckled.

"It's brioche bread, and I used heavy cream instead of milk. The comments said to try it, so I did. Turned out good as hell, if you ask me."

"Yes, it did, and I'm so proud of you. I'm glad you're learning to cook for yourself. I may not always be around to throw down in that kitchen—and your mama might not either. So it's a good thing you're taking some interest."

"You know what, Gigi? You're always talking about what I need to do. Let me tell you what you need to do. You need to hurry up and finish eating because I've got one more thing planned before we head out tonight."

Chapter Fifteen

"Ooohhh shit. What do you have up your sleeve now? And see, I don't want you spending all your money on me. When we first met, didn't you say you were broke? I don't like to count anyone's pockets, but I've been wondering how are you managing to take care of everything. All the bills, the food, the groceries... like how?"

"Now, is that really your business?"

"You're right. I'm sorry. I shouldn't have asked."

"Girl, I'm just playing with you! Do you not know when someone's being sarcastic?"

"Apparently not," We laughed.

"No, seriously though. I said the money my grandfather gave me was almost gone. The account he left me is damn near empty. But I never said that was my only account. I had bread before my grandpops passed. I told you I fix cars and do mechanic work on the side. I still do. Girl, I'm a hustler. That will never stop. Just like you have dreams, so do I."

"I hear that," I said, giving him a fist bump. "I'm done, as you can see."

He removed my plate and tray and took them to the kitchen.

"I need you to stay right where you are. Don't move," he said firmly.

"Umm, can I at least go wash my hands? I need to get this syrup off. Getting it on your couch is the last thing I want to do."

"Nope, you can't go wash your hands. Just stay right there and try not to touch anything!" Echo yelled from his bedroom.

"Okay," I yelled back, giggling. "What is this boy up to?

About five minutes later, he called from his room and told me to close my eyes. Since he hadn't led me wrong yet, I trusted him and did what he asked without rebuttal.

A couple of minutes later, I felt a warm rag sliding between my fingers. Then I felt him grab my feet.

"Keep your eyes closed," he said again.

It was hard, but I obeyed. Then, I felt warm water

surrounding my toes. He had submerged my feet in a foot basin.

"You can open your eyes now," he said cheerfully.

I did and was floored. He'd set up a pedicure caddy and a small stool for himself. He reached into the trolley, grabbed bath salts, and poured them into the water.

I sat there stunned. I didn't even know what to say, so I didn't say anything.

My grandmother had told me how Jesus washed His disciples' feet, and because of that, I couldn't help but weep silently.

He smiled at me so adoringly. And for the first time since I entered those doors, I felt bad because now I understood he'd been showing his love for me all along. Somehow, I'd missed the cues. It was so strong in that moment, I couldn't help but acknowledge it. His words always matched his actions. And for that, I knew, beyond a shadow of a doubt, that he loved me.

I was now more conflicted than I had ever been. I was scheduled to take my ASVAB test on Monday and had planned to tell him I was leaving as soon as I got my results. Now, I had no idea how to do that without breaking his heart.

I became emotional as he rubbed my feet so gently. He then cut and filed my toenails. When he was done, he pulled out five polish colors and told me to choose one. I picked white, and he painted my toes.

The whole experience was nothing short of amazing. Echo had just given me my first pedicure.

"Now where did you learn how to do this? Or is this something you've always done for the ladies in your life?" I asked, facetiously.

"YouTube," he laughed.

By the time he finished, I was halfway asleep. He had me in a complete state of relaxation, as only he could.

Then, the doorbell rang. I got up to answer it, but he ordered me to stay put...again.

At the door, I heard him say, "Yes, come on in. You're at the right place."

A nice lady entered the living room and introduced herself.

"Hello, Gigi. I'm your massage therapist for today. Mr. Black booked a one-and-a-half-hour massage for you. Would you mind showing me where you'd like me to set up?"

Glancing at Echo, he just smiled and turned his head. Shaking mine, I led her to the entertainment room.

As she set up, I returned to the living room, ready to fuss at Echo for spending so much money, only to realize that he and Sheba were gone.

Back in the entertainment room, she was ready to begin.

God definitely heard me say I couldn't relax, because He immediately remedied that. Miss Angela had magic hands that had me snoring like a nine-year-old pug on the table.

Once she completed the service, she cleaned up, took her equipment out to her car, then came back to say goodbye.

I tried to tip her, but she refused. She said, "Your boyfriend took very good care of me."

I thanked her for her services, and she left.

This had been the absolute best birthday I'd ever had. I felt like a brand-new person, but still deeply aware of the decisions I had to make. It was tearing me apart, but I decided that I wouldn't focus on that today.

I would enjoy myself the best I could. The massage mellowed me out so much that I set my alarm for four and trekked back upstairs to take a much-needed nap.

Chapter Sixteen

My alarm blared, startling me awake, and I jumped up immediately. I was excited, like a kid in a candy store. I started with a shower, then moved on to my hair. I put in flexi rods because I wanted that sexy, bouncy curl look, and I beat my face the best way I knew how.

I'd never been a big makeup girly, but I had everything I needed laid out in front of me. Taking a page from Echo's book, I turned on a YouTube tutorial and followed along. I didn't do half bad, and for the first time in a long time, I felt beautiful.

I slathered my body in white jasmine vanilla shea butter, then added the little accessories he'd bought for me. Finally, I slipped into my dress, shoes, grabbed my purse, and spritzed on a couple of squirts of perfume. He had such great taste. Everything he picked out matched perfectly. Running back to the bathroom, I added the finishing touches to my hair, a little more lip gloss, and just like that... I was ready for the night.

By the time I was done, it was 5:30 on the dot. I opened my bedroom door and peeked down the stairs. I was met with silence. My nerves kicked in. Did he forget about me? Did he not come home?

Then I heard his voice call out, "Bring your ass on down those stairs and let me see that dress."

I ran...almost tripping because me and heels didn't really get along like that. But when I made it to the bottom of the stairs, there he was, looking as debonair as ever. Echo had always been fine, but tonight he was giving grown man, protector, provider fine.

He took one look at me, smiled, and said, "You look beautiful, Gigi. I mean absolutely gorgeous. Come on, let's ride."

"We have to stop by your mother's, right?"

"Yeah. It'll only take a minute."

Grabbing my hand, he led me out the front door to the Hellcat. As usual, he opened my door and sitting in the passenger seat was a small box. Eager to open it, I flopped down and started to unwrap it. He stopped me before I could fully open it.

"Wait. Don't open that yet. I want you to put it in your purse and open it later."

"Aww, Echo, seriously? Just in case you didn't know, patience isn't one of my virtues."

"I hate that for you," he whispered as we pulled out the driveway.

We breezed past the gate and headed to his mother's house. Pulling into an affluent neighborhood in Roseville, we arrived at a beautiful home. One that rivaled the mansion Jah lived in.

"Gigi, come in for a minute. My mother will be mad if I have you sitting in the car. It'll only take a second."

I hopped out the car, looking cute. Ready to see the inside of this gorgeous house and his mom. She'd been nothing but kind to me, and she didn't know me from a stray house cat. The least I could do was say hello.

He walked up to the door and rang the bell. When it opened, his mother stretched out her arms and said, "Hey girl, I haven't seen you in a little bit. How have you been?"

"I'm good, Ma Dukes. Did your son tell you all the things he did for me today? He's trying to spoil me rotten."

Grabbing my hand, she mumbled, "No chile, he didn't tell me anything." Then, pulling me inside, she added, "Why don't you tell me all about it?"

We rounded the corner.

“SURPRISE!!!” Was being screamed at me from every direction.

I looked at all the smiling faces and immediately burst into tears. I buried my face into Echo’s chest. Looking up at him, I asked through sobs, “How did you know? I didn’t even tell you.”

“Girl, we live together. Did you really think you were gonna get away without me knowing your birthday? You leave that ID laying everywhere. I’m just trying to figure out why you didn’t mention it but we’ll talk about that later.”

His family members came from everywhere. His little sister walked up, handed me a small present, kissed me on the cheek, and told me I looked pretty like a Disney Princess.

Kneeling a little, I said, “Well, thank you, pudding. That’s the nicest thing anyone has ever said to me.”

“You’re welcome!” she chirped, before running off.

I didn’t know a single one of these people, but I could feel I was surrounded by love. They hugged me, complimented me, and doted on me like I had never been doted on before. I was so overwhelmed by their warmth that I didn’t even notice the beautiful decorations or the banner that read GENEVIÈVE in all caps hanging from the banister.

They really went all out for little old me. There were

flowers and candles everywhere. A caterer had been hired, and the spread they laid out was fit for royalty. Right in the center sat a huge cake shaped like a water bottle and all I could do was laugh.

This was truly one of the best days of my life.

Chapter Seventeen

Once the party ended and everyone said their goodbyes, I tried to help his mama clean up. She refused my help, stating that she hired people for that. Shooing me away, she told me to go sit down somewhere. I didn't need to be told twice. My feet were killing me, and I took my shoes off with no shame.

"There you are," Echo said, rounding the corner. "I've been looking all over for you. You ready to ride out?"

"I am, but please don't tell me there are any more surprises. I don't think I could take another one. Boy, you've got me exhausted."

"No, Lil Thugger. That was it. I'm gonna get you home so you can rest."

We waved our goodbyes, Echo picked up my shoes, and carried me to the car.

"Today has been a day," I said as we cruised down the highway. "Now you've got to tell me...how long have you been planning all of this?"

"For a while, honestly. I'm just glad we pulled it off without you suspecting anything. You've kinda been in your own world lately, and I wasn't sure if the timing was right."

"I know. I've got a lot on my mind, and I've just been trying to figure out how to navigate it all."

"Well, Gigi, tell me what's on your mind because I never know. You're doing well in school. You're about to graduate. What could possibly have you in your head like that?"

"Don't worry about it now, Echo. Let's just leave the night on a high note. It was too good of a day to fuck it up with my issues."

"If you say so. But I hope you realize it's okay not to be okay sometimes. No one's gonna judge you for having a bad day or a bad week, in your case," he said, kissing the inside of my wrist.

"Shut up. I'm not that bad. I just be chilling and trying to mind my business, that's all. Sometimes I disconnect from everything and everyone but that's been a coping mechanism for me. In the past, I had to."

"And now you don't. You're good with me, and you can talk to me about anything. Good or bad," he uttered.

"I know. But some things are better left unsaid."

"Better for who?" he asked as he covered my hand with his.

He pulled into the driveway and parked in front of the garage and killed the motor.

"I know I told you I was done with surprises," he said, "but I promise this is the last one. I kept you busy today so you wouldn't notice the Maxima was gone. I've been trying to keep you out of this damn garage."

He hit the clicker, and the garage door lifted, revealing his final surprise.

The Maxima was now pink and wrapped to perfection. Hopping out of the car, I screamed, "When in the hell did you find time to do all this, Echo?!"

"I have my ways," he said with a grin. "It's been gone since early this morning. My homeboy hooked it up. He brought it back while we were at the party."

I walked around the car slowly, falling more in love with every step. With him *and* the car. The inside had been cleaned and detailed to the point it looked brand new. A pink monogrammed cup sat in the cupholder. Pink dice hung from the mirror, along with pink steering wheel covers, floor mats and seat covers. And engraved on the dash were the words Lil Thugger. I was floored.

I grabbed him by the neck, pulled him close, and whispered, "Thank you for everything," with tears in my eyes.

"Echo, I haven't cried this much in my life and all happy tears at that. You are truly one of a kind."

"I love you," slipped from my lips before I could even think.

He pulled back, eyes wide. "Did you just say you love me?"

I stammered. "Umm... Umm... I, I—"

He wrapped his arms around my waist and kissed me so deeply and passionately that my knees buckled.

"I love you too, Gigi," he whispered, scooping me up and carrying me into the house.

We didn't make it past the couch. He ripped my dress off and even though I was caught up in the moment, I covered my body to hide my marks, my past. He gently moved my hands away.

"Gigi, you are the most beautiful thing that I've ever laid eyes on. You are flawless to me. You don't have to be ashamed of anything."

His words lit a fire inside of me and my pelvis started to radiate with heat. A new feeling for me and I liked it. He undressed in front of me, dropping his clothes piece by piece revealing what had been in store for me all along. Perfection. From the looks of his member, I could tell that he'd been wanting this for a long time.

Standing bare skinned in front of me, his lips found mine again. He licked his fingers and slid down to find my center. I wanted to stop him, but I didn't. I couldn't. I was completely enthralled in a way that was unfamiliar to me. He had my full attention, and I wanted more. More of this feeling, more of him.

My body leaned into him, until we were chest to chest. He twiddled my nipple as he rocked my clit until a sensation and feeling that I'd never felt before took over my body. Whatever it was, it was powerful and made me forget that I was standing.

My knees buckled again. Weak, I searched for the couch to sit down to recover, but he doesn't let me. He gently laid me back and began to eat my pussy like he was broke, the rent was due, and I was the landlord.

He devoured me and I couldn't stop quivering. His tongue found my asshole and that seriously had me rethinking my life. *What is this man doing to me? I don't know if I can take anymore*. Just when I thought I couldn't, he came up for air, pressed his lips into mine and slid deep into my center.

My mouth opened involuntarily. The sheer girth and length sent waves of pleasure through my entire body. My hips got the memo and started to rock to meet his. We both moaned in ecstasy. Our body's danced horizontally, while he seemed to caress every inch of me. I began to feel as if I would short circuit.

"Oooh shit, Echo, I moaned. It's so good baby. Please don't stop."

"I won't, I promise. I love you Gigi," he confessed as he whispered and nibbled on my ear. "Do you know that I love you so much?" He muttered as he stroked my pussy with intention, with perfection.

"I love you too Echo, I contended as our bodies became one. We were intertwined. One heart, one soul, one body as we erupted in such a beautiful way.

There was no fear present, no pain, no anxiousness. Only pleasure sharing and complete submission.

Panting, we both relaxed. Trying to catch our breath. I felt his body loosen. He became lighter, diluted and I became the same.

I'd had sex before. Too many times to count, but it never felt like *that*. My body never reacted like *that*. *That* felt natural, enjoyable... *that* felt like love.

We laid in each other's arms and drifted off to sleep.

Chapter Eighteen

Poor Sheba. She must've been mortified to see what her mama and papa were doing to each other last night. We were so busy trying to rip each other's clothes off that we completely forgot to take her out for her nightly walk. At some point during the night, Echo must've let her out of her crate because I woke up to her licking me in the face.

Exhausted from the day before, we decided to make it a lazy Sunday. Knowing that I had the test tomorrow left me feeling uneasy, and uncertainty haunted me. After last night, I even questioned whether I should move forward with my plans.

Still, I tried not to focus on that. Echo and I laid around and just enjoyed each other's company. After lunch, we decided to take a nap. Just as sleep found me, I was startled awake by a knock at the door. As I rose from the couch, the knocking grew louder.

I glanced over at Echo and he was sound asleep. My first instinct was to wake him up to answer the door, since this was his house. But then I remembered how he'd gotten onto me about calling it that.

It's my house too, I reminded myself as I ran to open the door and found his father standing on the doorstep.

"Is my son in there?" he asked.

"Yes, sir. He's asleep. Would you like me to wake him up?"

"Yes, please. It's urgent."

"Would you like to come in?"

"No, I'm good out here. Just have him come out and talk to me."

"Okay, if you insist," I said, closing the door. As I turned around, I heard Echo's voice behind me.

"Who is it?"

"It's your father. He says he needs to speak to you and it's urgent."

He headed out the front door while I laid back down on the couch. I tried to return to sleep, but the urgency in his father's voice had me worried. What if something happened to his mom or sister?

I sat up, restless, and waited for him to return.

About thirty minutes passed before he came back in.

He sat down quietly and stared at me like he was trying to read my soul.

"Is everything okay? Are you going to say something, or are you just going to stare at me?"

"Yes, Genevieve. Everything's fine."

A wave of worry washed over me. He *never* called me Genevieve. Something was definitely wrong. But I didn't press the issue because he never pressed me when I didn't want to talk.

He laid back on the couch and stared at the ceiling in silence.

I didn't know what was said between him and his father, but something had shifted. The energy in the room felt heavy. He hadn't said more than three words to me since he came back, so I got up and went to the bedroom.

I stayed in there the rest of the day until it was time to take Sheba for her walk. When he saw me grab the leash, he asked if he could come along.

"Sure, why not," I said. I slipped on my shoes and headed out the door.

We walked in silence for a while before I asked, "Are you really not going to tell me what your father said? He must've said something upsetting because you've been eerily quiet."

"He did say some things that have me concerned, but it's nothing for you to worry about. Kinda like you always tell me...no need to ruin the day with my bullshit, right? I'm just taking a page out of your book."

"If you say so, Echo."

We kept walking in silence, and just as we were almost home, he turned to me. "Did you really mean what you said last night?"

"What are you referring to, Echo? A lot happened yesterday. I said a lot."

"You said you love me last night. Do you really love me?"

"When have you ever known me to lie to you? If I said I love you, then I love you. Why would you even ask me that?" I asked, frustrated.

"Just trying to see something," he quipped.

"What do you mean, *trying to see something*? What exactly are you trying to see?" I snapped.

"Gigi, I've learned not to ask you too many questions because you shut down. I'm afraid that if I do, I won't get a straight answer, or you'll just break down in tears. Neither makes me feel good. So, I'm just gonna shut the fuck up and leave it alone."

"Echo, what is happening right now? This isn't like you. Even your tone sounds off so I know that something is wrong. I can't force you to tell me what it is, just like you can't force me... but I know that I'm not crazy.

Something has got you in your feelings but just know

that you never have to question whether or not I love you, because I do. I don't say those three words lightly, and I damn sure don't just throw them around to anyone."

Bucking his eyes, he asked, "Are you sure about that?"

"Okay, now you're starting to piss me off. I don't like that passive-aggressive shit. If you have something to say or ask me, just say it. Don't make me feel like I'm losing my mind when I know I'm not. You always say I can tell you anything. That you're open. That you don't judge. Now you're being standoffish, and I don't understand why, but it's cool.

When we get back, I think I'm going to skip dinner and just go to bed. I've got school tomorrow, and I need rest. Maybe you can order takeout or go grab something to eat if you're hungry," I said as we stepped into the house.

I unclipped Sheba's leash and headed upstairs. Once in my room, I began to replay everything from last night to this morning. Yesterday was absolutely perfect and today started that way too but it damn sure didn't end like it.

Something was definitely going on with Echo, but I couldn't let myself stress over it. I was already dealing with enough.

As I got ready for tomorrow, I reminded myself that this decision was about me, my future. I'd gone back and forth about the Air Force, but I finally came to the conclusion that this was the best move. If I truly wanted to make something of myself, I had to do this and I couldn't worry about how anyone else would feel about it.

I hopped in and out the shower, threw on my pajamas, and slid under the covers. Letting thoughts of all the opportunities ahead ease my mind. Finally, I drifted into a peaceful sleep.

Chapter Nineteen

Echo woke me up at 5:00 a.m. to let me know he was leaving early, saying he had a couple of vehicles to work on before heading to his job. Still uneasy about how he'd acted yesterday, I just said, "Okay," rolled over, and went back to sleep.

I shouldn't have done that. I overslept and was going to be late if I didn't hurry. I jumped in the shower, bathed, brushed my teeth, fixed my hair, grabbed a bagel, and rushed out the door.

Thankfully, I made it to school in time. Shortly after I arrived, the Air Force recruiter picked me up and took me to the testing site. He'd told me ahead of time that it might be an all-day process, so I kept that in mind. I didn't know what to expect, but it turned out to be easier than I'd imagined.

Since the results were immediate, the recruiter let me know that I'd scored extremely high and had the privilege of choosing my job.

I chose Aerospace Physiology. Before I left the office, we scheduled my MEPS visit. After that, I would be sworn in and given a leave date. I looked forward to every step of the process. It was exciting and nerve-racking all at once.

Done with testing, the recruiter dropped me off at my car. There were still a couple of hours left in the school day, but I was heading home. On my way, my gas light came on, forcing me to stop and fill up. I wasn't about to end up stranded on the side of anyone's highway.

I pulled into a gas station, hopped out, and was immediately accosted by a group of guys asking for my number.

I didn't want to say the wrong thing. I'd read too many stories of women being shot for turning men down. Thankfully, I swerved through the crowd unharmed and made it into the store, damn near shaking.

The clerk, a woman, asked if I was okay.

"No ma'am, I am not. I don't want to go back out there. Is there anything you can do? Can't you make them leave or call the police?"

"Girl, do you see how rowdy they are?" she replied. "Ain't shit I can do about them. I've complained to the owner several times and suggested he put up a 'No Loitering' sign, but even he said it wouldn't make a difference.

Those niggas hang out here for hours at a time. No telling when they'll leave."

"Well, I'm not going back out there. They're too damn aggressive for me. You need to tell the owner he needs to hire security or something. I'm never coming back here again."

"You're a beautiful girl. Don't you have a man you can call?" She asked.

My mind instantly went to Echo, but after how he was acting, I wasn't sure that was a good idea. I sat down on some milk crates and waited, hoping they'd leave.

As I waited, the cowbell above the door rang and in walked the infamous Rolla.

Praying he didn't see me, I dropped my head into my lap and tried to become invisible.

"Gigi? I say, Gigi, is that you over there, girl? Girl, get yo ass up and give me a hug! I been askin' your mama about you, and she don't know shit. She's been worried sick."

"Is that so?" I said, raising my head. "You can tell my mother that I'm fine. No thanks to her. And I wouldn't hug you with that lady's arms," I muttered, pointing at the clerk.

"Gigi, you need to let that shit go. I have. You cracked two of my ribs, and I'm good, baby. Life is life. Good and bad shit happens. Just so you know, your mama loves you.

Hell, *you're* the reason she's sober. Did you hear me, Gigi? Your mama is sober. She don't fuck with none of that shit no more. No pills, no powder. She still has a drink now and then, but she's off the hard shit, babygirl. No lie."

"Rolla, first of all, what I did to you doesn't even begin to compare to a lifetime of abuse from my mother and niggas like you. Don't *ever* say that stupid shit again. You're the last muthafucka I'd take advice from. You like to fuck little girls, for God's sake. That disqualifies you from being any kind of reliable source. And as far as my mother being sober, I'll believe it when I see it. She's pulled the sober shit before, and it lasted all of three days. I've accepted who she is, and I'm moving on with my life."

"Hold on now, Gigi, I—"

Cutting him off mid-sentence, I said loudly, "Don't say shit else to me, Rolla. Just leave me alone. If you really want to help me, clear a path so I can get the fuck out of here."

He went outside, dapped up a few of the guys, and seconds later looked back into the store, waving for me to come out. I peeked out. The parking lot was empty.

Nodding at him, I hopped back into the Maxima.

As I pulled off, Rolla shouted, "I'm sorry, Gigi!" from the parking lot.

I tossed up a peace sign and peeled off. I still needed

gas badly, so I drove to a little mom-and-pop gas station on the outskirts—far away from the fuckery of the city.

With a full tank, I headed home. Echo was in the driveway detailing the Hellcat. As I got out of the car, I spoke, then walked inside. Sheba was running around in the yard, having the time of her life.

As I reached the front door, Echo stopped me and asked if I'd stay outside with him for a bit.

"Echo, normally I wouldn't mind, but my nerves are shot. Some niggas ran up on me at the gas station, and I felt like I was going to pass out. I'm a little shaken up and I just want to lie down."

"Wait. What happened?"

I told him the whole story. He turned red all over, and I could practically see steam coming from his ears. He dropped the sponge, ran over to me, grabbed my hand, called for Sheba, and led us both into the house. We sat down on the couch.

"Are you okay?"

"Yes, Echo, I'm fine."

"What I want to know is why you didn't call me?" He asked.

"And just what were you going to do? There were like ten of them. They would've eaten your ass alive, and I couldn't have that on my conscience. Besides, you didn't seem like you wanted to be bothered yesterday. You seemed really irritated, and I don't know how to handle you shutting down on me."

"Okay, Gigi, yes, I was a little short with you last night. But I'm okay today. I do need to talk to you about something."

"I need to talk to you too, Echo."

Chapter Twenty

"I was going to wait until everything was finalized, but I've got a feeling you may already know something. In that case, I want you to hear it from me. I don't need anybody else telling my story and fucking it up."

Noticing my palms had begun to sweat, I dried them and grabbed his hand.

"Echo, first I want to say that these past few months we've spent together have been life-changing for me. This is the first time I've consistently been in a healthy environment. The first time I've been able to relax without fear of being bothered or attacked."

"Attacked?" he repeated, looking confused.

"Yes, attacked. Please let me finish, Echo, because if I don't get this out now, I might never get through it. You've always said I seem quiet and reserved, like I'm always lost in thought. And you're right. I always have something on my mind.

A past like mine is hard to forget. The reason I didn't want you to see my mother in Walmart that night is because I'm ashamed of her. I was afraid that if you saw her, you'd see her in me.

My mother isn't a good person. I don't think there's a single point in my life where she ever was. She's a drug addict and a prostitute and has been for most of my life. Well at least of the parts that I can remember.

The night we met at the store, I had just cracked one of her tricks in the ribs for trying to sleep with me."

"Wait..." he said, stunned.

"No, Echo. I need to finish. She used to sell me to men for drugs and money. That night, I'd had enough. I was either going to kill somebody in that house or kill myself, so I had to go.

I've been used, abused, and neglected since I was a child. I don't know my father. I never have. She never told me who he was. She probably doesn't even know herself."

"Gigi, you don't have to do this if you don't want to."

"No, but I *want* to. I *need* to. Echo, I am broken and unhealed in so many ways. Sometimes it feels like I'm outside my body, watching you put me back together. Like you're healing me right in front of my eyes. It's scary because I've never trusted a man in my life. Hell, I *couldn't*. But I now know that I can trust you. And that's why it hurts me and makes it so hard for me to tell you that...I, I...I'm leaving Roseville."

"Leaving? What do you mean you're leaving? Where are you going, Gigi?"

"To the Air Force. I took the ASVAB and scored pretty high, so it won't be long now. The recruiters offered me the opportunity, and I want to take it. I've been hell-bent on getting out of this town because I didn't feel like there was anything here for me, but now I see that there is. *You*. However, I know I need to deal with my issues and get help. That's what I plan to do."

"What kind of help do you need, Gigi? I thought that's what we were doing here, helping each other. I've got your back, and you've got mine."

"We are helping each other. But I'm afraid that someone like me, with the past I have, will only end up breaking your heart. I'm not okay. I know I've got a long way to go, and I don't want to hurt you. I know now that you love me, and I love you too, but I also know I need to have a weekly spot on somebody's couch. I need therapy. I need to heal. I also need to learn how to take care of myself. My life has been a struggle since day one, and I'm tired of living like that."

"Wait, Gigi, just wait. You've got it all wrong. We take

care of *each other*, don't we? It's not a one-way street. You do just as much for me as I do for you. I've told you time and time again, I don't mind taking care of you. You give me purpose. I don't understand why you're trying to bounce. What am I supposed to do without you?" Sadness was etched across his face.

"Please don't do this, Echo. Please. I already feel terrible for leaving. I didn't know I could feel this way about someone. I know now that I love you, but I also believe in Divine timing. If we're truly meant to be together, fate and destiny will make it happen."

Shaking his head no, he offers, "Listen, with your grades, you could easily get a scholarship to one of these schools in Bama. That way we could be close. I'd drive to wherever you are. Just... please stay close."

"I guess I should've considered your feelings because they do matter, but since we're not in a quote-unquote relationship, I didn't think I needed to. And *that's* what I mean, Echo. I don't know how to love. Not properly, anyway."

He put his head in his hands and sat in silence. The quiet between us was deafening.

Finally, he raised his head and said, "Gigi... my father told me yesterday that one of his friends noticed you. He knew your mother and told my father about how she got down. He recognized you at the party. He told me a little about your past and said he was trying to save me from the little fast-tailed girl who was preying on his son.

But I knew better. You don't ask me for anything. I've seen you do nothing but go to school and come home. I'll admit, the things he said had me a little heated, but now I'm thankful you chose to share your truth with me. It all makes sense now, and I feel so bad. Nobody should have to grow up like that. But if anything, it makes me respect and love you even more because you didn't let it change your heart.

Gigi, the love I have for you is real. No one and nothing will ever compare to you. With that being said, I love you enough to let you go out there and become the best version of yourself. Just promise me you won't forget about me. Promise me we'll keep in touch and that we'll never lose this connection we have. If you've made your decision to leave, I won't try to stop you. I just ask that we spend whatever time we have left loving on each other, making the most of these final days. Can you promise me that?"

"Yes, Echo. I promise," I whispered as I cupped his face and kissed his lips.

Looking up, I noticed the tears in his eyes. They matched the ones in mine.

From that day until I left for basic training, we were joined at the hip. We did everything together. We began sleeping in the same bed and made love every chance we got. We bonded like no other, and I knew without a shadow of a doubt, that he was my soulmate, my person.

A month later, in May, I graduated from high school. Echo's parents threw a graduation party for me and one of his cousins. Shortly after that, Echo and Sheba stood by my side as I loaded the bus for basic training. My eyes were full of tears and my head full of worry. I was leaving Roseville behind to chase a better future. It was so bittersweet.

Chapter Twenty-One

PRESENT DAY -2025

Basic training wasn't as hard as I thought it would be. Running from tricks and taking Sheba on those long walks had built up my stamina. Honestly, it was a cakewalk. I excelled at everything thrown my way.

After completing basic, Echo and his family were there to see me graduate. He tapped me out, and I cried tears of joy. They were proud of me, and I was proud of myself. I'd met one of my first major goals, and it wouldn't be my last.

I became a goal digger and an overachiever. It was like I'd gone from competing with the world to competing with myself. I wanted to live out loud simply because I hadn't been able to before. I craved new experiences, adventures, and connections. I became well-traveled, living in places I'd never imagined. While in the Air Force, I forged meaningful relationships and connections with tons of amazing people. I even tried dating a time or two but ended up comparing every man to Echo. There was no comparison.

Echo and I kept in touch for the first couple of years, but eventually the phone calls and letters became fewer and fewer until they stopped altogether. I missed him, but I didn't trip. We were both young. And while I loved him with every fiber of my being, it would've been foolish to think he'd wait around for me. I never wanted him to do that anyway. He deserved a full and abundant life. As I'd said that day on the couch, if we were meant to be, we would be. I left it in God's hands.

While in the Air Force, I attended intense therapy and was diagnosed with PTSD and generalized anxiety disorder. Therapy taught me how to control my emotions and how to deal with and move past the traumas of my past. It helped me tremendously.

It had been ten years since I left Roseville and everything behind to join the military. I'd now decided it was time to start the next chapter of my life.

Betting on myself, I left the Air Force. Departing with an honorable discharge. This was the end of my military career and the beginning of my journey into real estate.

A dear friend and colleague pointed me in the right direction. After completing the coursework, I passed the real estate licensing exam with flying colors. In addition to real estate, I'm also in the process of launching a nonprofit to help teenage girls and boys escape volatile environments.

With the knowledge and connections I've gained, deciding to move back to Roseville just seemed right. If any town needs help, it's mine. Since getting out of the military, I've visited a few times to scout potential homes. On my most recent visit, I made the move official. I closed on my new home a week ago. It's a five-bedroom, three-bath house, and at twenty-eight years old… I'm THAT BITCH.

My furniture and belongings are set to arrive in less than a week, so in the meantime, a nice quaint Airbnb is where I reside.

My new home is in a great part of town with a solid school system and fantastic potential for real estate development which is right up my alley.

In the short time I've been back, I can already see that a lot hasn't changed. But I plan on changing that.

Being back home stirs up a lot. Both good and bad memories. Thanks to therapy, I try to focus more on the good. The positive thoughts almost make me want to hop in my brand-new C300 Mercedes and ride over to Echo's house to see if he's still around. But I resist, not wanting to interfere with whatever he may have going on.

Instead of focusing on dating or men in general, I'm

pouring everything into building my career and leveling up. I've got this new house, this new car, and I need the means to maintain it, so I get to work immediately. Showing houses day in and day out. Business is booming.

I feel great about every aspect of my life, except one. The one thing I haven't made peace with is my relationship with my mother. Now that I'm older, I understand that drug addiction is a sickness. People often do terrible things to feed that habit. Forgiveness was granted years ago to someone that may not even be sorry, but we never reconnected. I need that for my mental health and closure.

I never forgot what Rolla told me...that my mother was sober. So, after some soul searching. I drive by to see for myself. As I approach the house, my heart drops. It's boarded up with a sign saying it's been condemned.

Panic rises in my chest and a warm sensation covers my head.

What if I'm too late?

What if she's dead?

Pulling over, I park, taking slow, deep breaths. Just like my therapist taught me. I haven't had to use these techniques in ages, but I was aware coming back to Roseville could bring this kind of emotional weight.

As I'm breathing, there's a knock at my window. Startled, I let it down and a jit leans in and asks, "You looking for someone?"

"Yes. A lady named Shanice Parker used to live here. Do you know what happened to her?" I ask.

"I know Ms. Shanice. She was a real nice lady from what I knew. She moved about two years ago. A tornado came through and messed up a lot of houses around here. A lot of people had to leave. I'm sorry, I don't know where she went."

"Oh my God, that's so sad. But thank you for telling me."

"No problem, Ma'am," he said with a smile before walking away.

I roll up my window and pull off. After receiving the information regarding my Mama, I head back to my Airbnb to change. Deciding to take myself out to dinner, I search Google for restaurants that have popped up since I've been gone. I've been all work and no play lately. It's time to get back in the mix.

Being a hermit isn't my thing anymore. I love being outside. Roseville might not have tons of fine dining, but the food is still top-tier. I've eaten at some of the best restaurants in the world, but nothing compares to Southern cooking.

I had a taste for soul food but somehow end up at an Italian restaurant. I order Chicken Principessa, bruschetta, and a split of red wine. Eating alone used to bother me, but now I actually enjoy it. Most people find it intimidating. I think it makes me look mysterious. Sexy, even.

The food is amazing, and I get full quickly. I ask for a to-go box, pack my food, pay my tab, and head to the nearest bar.

I arrive and haven't even been on the barstool two minutes before the men start in. One by one, I turn them down. I start thinking maybe sitting at the bar isn't the best idea.

Looking for some privacy, I find a chair tucked in the cut and sit down. When the bartender comes by, I order a French 75 and tell her to keep them coming. Three drinks later, I close out my tab and head for the door.

As I'm walking out, I hear a voice say,"Gigi, are you seriously going to walk past me like you don't know me?"

"Girl, I didn't even recognize you. Those drinks in there are strong as hell. I'm sorry. Hey, Tasia," I say, giving her a sideways hug.

I can tell she's surprised. The last time we were this close, I almost rocked her shit. But I'm over all that now. All is well.

She asks if I'm just visiting, and I simply say no. I may have forgiven her, but I still don't trust her. You can never trust a bitch that's jealous of you. That didn't come from therapy, that little nugget came from my mama.

"Well, have you seen Mama Shanice since you've been

back? Girl, every time I go by there, she asks about you. My granny and your mom are in the same facility. You know, Whispering Oaks, the nursing home."

"*Nursing home?*" I whisper to myself. *My mother is in a nursing home.*

"Umm, yeah. I planned to visit her tomorrow. I just got in," I lie. Knowing damn well that I had no idea where she was until now.

"Oh, okay. Well, it was good to see you, Gigi. You look great."

"You too, Tasia. I hope you're doing well. Maybe I'll see you around."

Smiling and waving goodbye, I wobble to my car. Thank God my Airbnb is only a mile away. Those drinks have me bent. They definitely don't skimp on the liquor in that place. Next time, I'll stop at two instead of three.

I make it to my temporary home safely and start undressing as soon as I walk in. If I'm home and comfortable, I prefer to be naked. The liquor is hitting me hard, and I immediately start kicking myself. I have six houses to show tomorrow.

I hop in the shower, then come out to put my leftovers in the fridge. I sit down to watch TV until the TV starts watching me.

Chapter Twenty-Two

I wake up at 6:30 sharp to start my day. I've become a stickler for doing things in a timely manner, and I rarely deviate from my schedule. My first showing is at 8:00 AM, but the house is right around the corner. I don't have far to travel but I like to arrive early. This gives me time to set up and make sure everything is in perfect condition before my potential buyers arrive.

I feel tense this morning, so while in the shower, I decide to take care of that. Grabbing my rose, I put it to work. It never fails me. Within three minutes, I'm bucking like a Brahman bull.

Coming down off my pleasure high, I grab a towel and exit the shower. The first house I'm showing today is in a very prominent neighborhood, so I dig into the closet for one of the many nice suits I've acquired over the years and get dressed. I choose a yellow vintage Chanel skirt suit with Christian Louboutin heels. I pair it with my mother-of-pearl Van Cleef necklace and Cartier Juste un Clou and Love bracelets. Then, I top it all off with my Donna Born in Roma Valentino perfume.

I've learned that not only must you have money to make money, it doesn't hurt to look like money too.

I begin my day, showing house after house, receiving offers on two of them. At this rate, I'm destined to have my name on a billboard. I return to the office to start the paperwork and begin reading my emails. My colleague, Angel, advises that a Ms. Baptiste is interested in viewing the last house I just left. I let her know I'm done for the day but would be happy to show it tomorrow morning. She agrees, and I pencil her in.

Done handling business, I put Whispering Oaks into my GPS, praying the whole way there. I ask God to give me the wisdom and strength needed for this encounter. I also ask Him to bridle my tongue. I'm not going there to argue, just to gain understanding... if at all possible.

As I approach the facility, I realize it doesn't look familiar at all. It's so rundown that I'm almost scared to walk inside but I didn't get this far to turn around. This is something I need to do.

Walking into the building, I'm greeted by a sweet lady named Mrs. Underwood. I tell her I'm there to see Shanice

Parker. She checks the book, gives me a visitor's pass, and tells me her room number.

As I stroll down the hallway, my heart begins to race, and my palms start sweating. *Damn, this is pathetic.*

I haven't even made it to her room yet, and I'm already panicking. Looking around at my surroundings, I see tons of wheelchairs, the smell of piss hangs heavy in the air, and the nurses and CNAs are standing around doing absolutely nothing, except staring me down.

"Is there somebody in particular you're looking for, ma'am?" one nurse asks.

"There is, but I have the room number. Thank you anyhow," I say, continuing my trek. It feels like I've been walking for ten minutes when, in truth, it's only been one.

I arrive at the door and freeze. I try to force myself to go in, but my feet won't budge. I just can't.

I thought all the money I spent on therapy had paid off, until now. Faced with this situation, I crumble. I turn around, put one foot in front of the other, and practically run out of the building.

I'm not ready to see her. I think I'm still in shock. A nursing home. My mom is in a fucking nursing home. And a terrible one at that. Running to my car, I get in and cry. Why couldn't she just be a good mom? Why couldn't she get right? If not for herself, then at least for me? And how the hell did she end up here? I need answers... but I don't have the courage to ask the questions.

Still sitting in the parking lot, I consult with my best friend, Google, to find a reputable therapist in the area. I need guidance, and badly. I call the first one with five stars and make an appointment. I tell them I need to see someone as soon as possible.

Once that's settled, I put my car in reverse and begin the journey back across town to my Airbnb.

Once inside, I disrobe and sit down, attempting to wrap my head around what just occurred. My previous therapist and I talked about this moment so many times. We even role-played it, exploring the best way to respond without causing strife for either of us.

Call me DJ Khaled, because apparently, I played myself.

Role-playing doesn't have shit on the real thing. I whipped into that parking lot like I could conquer the world. I was going to go in that room and let my mother know that she had me fucked up—in the kindest way, of course. She was going to apologize, explain her mindset at the time, and take accountability for her fuckups. I would finally feel like forgiving her hadn't been in vain.

Instead, I left feeling like the little girl who used to lie in her room night after night feeling scared, unsure, and unloved.

I don't know why I thought this would be easy. I feel weak and defeated, and I'm over it. I'll try again another time.

To take my mind off the fuckery that is my life, I put together a grocery list. I refuse to eat takeout all week and since I'm spoiled, I have them delivered. Once they arrive, I make myself a juicy steak with garlic mashed potatoes and a side salad.

I turn on *Cross* on Prime and watch that fine-ass Aldis Hodge. That man makes my pussy salivate and I show her some attention since she asked so nicely.

I search the bottom of my suitcase for my nine-inch dildo I've affectionately named Trevante. Trevante, coupled with my rose is a winning combination if I've ever seen one. I fuck myself and make myself cum so hard the neighbors probably know my name.

Once upon a time, sexual satisfaction meant nothing to me, but making love to Echo that first night changed everything. That was the first time in my life I experienced an orgasm.

Once you experience the big O, it's hard not to crave it. He taught me how to love and learn my own body. He also taught me how to please myself, which I'm grateful for because the only orgasms I've had since being with him were ones I gave myself.

As I said, no one compares and that includes sexually.

Echo could make me cum without even touching me. One look in his eyes and a squeeze of my thighs would have me bussin' major nuts. He was a bad man... in a good way.

He may have been young, but he fucked and handled my body like he had years of experience. That wasn't the case though. He confessed he'd only been with one person before me and that she was an older woman. She must've trained him well because he would have me howling. Whoever he's with now is blessed, because that dick game goes crazy. I smile to myself, fluff my pillows, and let sleep find me.

Chapter Twenty-Three

I only have two houses to show today, so I told myself I'd focus on speaking with investors for my non-profit. It's going to require a lot of legwork to get it off the ground, but I'm up for the challenge. I hate being idle for too long, so this will help keep me busy.

I get up and make a lox bagel to snack on while I scour the internet for grants and resources. My showing is at 8:00 a.m., which is in approximately one hour, so I bookmark my progress and begin getting ready.

Once I'm dressed, I grab my Louie, my laptop, and I'm ready to go. On my way out the door, I receive a call from the moving company letting me know that someone rescheduled and they wanted to know if I'd mind them bringing my things early.

Hell no is the answer. I don't mind at all. "Yesterday is

too soon," I say as I plop down in the Benz and take off toward the showing. They advise me that instead of Monday, they'll be bringing my things on Saturday. That's only two days away and I'm elated.

I phone the moving crew I had scheduled to help move my things from the Airbnb to the new house. I advise them that there's been a change of plans and that I'd need them earlier than expected. They're on board, and everything is moving in the right direction. Hanging up with them, I arrive in the driveway and notice someone is already here.

Here we go again with these overzealous-ass buyers.

I get out of the car with a smile on my face and extend my hand for a handshake. She grabs me and hugs me, saying she's a hugger. I am not, but I play it cool.

"My name is Genevieve Parker, but everyone calls me Gigi. I'll be showing you this beautiful home today. I apologize if there's anything out of order inside. I usually try to remedy that before my clients arrive, but it looks like you've beat me here."

"I'm sorry about that," she says. "I can be a bit eager. I've been riding past this house for weeks, and I just couldn't wait to get inside. I've been peeking through the windows, but the neighbors started looking concerned, so I went ahead and called to set up a viewing."

"I understand," I assure her. "I was the same way when I purchased my home. I couldn't wait to get inside either."

"Oh, where are my manners? My name is Giselle Baptiste. It's nice to meet you."

"Likewise. Now, let me get you inside."

Once we enter, we go through damn near every square foot of the place. She leaves no stone unturned. She even wants to get into the attic to see what kind of insulation is installed. I advise against it as there's no lighting up there, plus I'm not going to be responsible if her ass falls off that ladder. These are twenty-two-foot ceilings, and I can't have her risk that.

"My fiancé will come with me next time, so I'll have him go up there. He couldn't make it today because he had a business meeting. Before we leave, I need to schedule another viewing so he can be in on this. I love this house. I mean, I really love it, and I want it. He told me to pick out whatever I desired, and I do believe this is the one, Ms. Parker."

"So, are you saying you want to go ahead and put in an offer?"

"Yes," she says enthusiastically.

"Do you want to do this before or after you consult with your fiancé?"

"Before. Like I said, he told me I could get whatever I want, and I want this. You already have my info. The next time we meet, you'll get his, and we can get this ball rolling. How soon do you think we can move in?"

"That depends, Ms. Baptiste. Inspections, financing, closing costs, the sellers. There are a lot of wheels that have to turn to complete the process, but I'd say two months at the least."

"Oh, I'm thinking sooner than that. There will be no financing. We'll be purchasing this house cash."

"Okay. The asking price is three point five million dollars."

"Yes, I know. I told you, I've been stalking this house for a minute now. My fiancé is going to take care of it."

"Well, let's get this ball rolling. I'll let the seller know that you're meeting their asking price, so it shouldn't be long now."

"Fantastic! I'm so excited. I can't wait for him to see it. If he finishes his business meeting early, is there a chance we can return today?"

"Sure, that shouldn't be a problem. Here is my direct number," I hand her a business card. "Please text me and let me know what time works for you, and we'll meet back here."

"Sounds good!" she shrieks as she speed-walks out the door. "Bye, Ms. Parker. See you in a little while!"

Shaking my head, I close up and leave.

Shit, I'd probably skip off just like she did if I had a

man buying me an almost four-million-dollar home. Must be nice.

I hop in my car to burn some time until I hear from Ms. Adderall. Riding through some of my old stomping grounds, I visit my old high school and speak with a few of the teachers, especially the ones who encouraged me and kept me on my toes. They all seem happy for me, and even happier that I've decided to come back to Roseville to try and make a change.

I mention to a few of them the non-profit I'm working on, and one...Mrs. Graham, knows all about grant writing and offers to help.

While we're talking about the process, I receive a message from Ms. Baptiste, letting me know her fiancé will be free around 2:00 p.m. I agree to the time and continue what I was doing. I set a date to come after school next week so Mrs. Graham and I can get started.

Chapter Twenty-Four

Leaving the school with my stomach growling, I stop by a quaint little bistro to grab a bite until it's time for the second showing. The food is delicious and so is the man sitting in the booth next to me.

He is fine as frog hair, and I can't keep my eyes off him. He's looking at me too, so I get up, move over to his booth, and take a seat.

He looks up at me with a shocked expression before saying, "Well hi there, beautiful. Why don't you go ahead and sit down," he chuckles.

"I normally wouldn't have done that, but you were staring at me so hard I thought you'd burn a hole through me. I decided to get closer so you wouldn't strain your eyes. My name is Genevieve. What's yours?"

"I'm Olufemi. Most people just call me Femi. It proves too difficult for them to pronounce."

"No, Olufemi, it's not too difficult. People are just lazy, disrespectful, and don't care. I'm not going to call you Femi unless you prefer it. I'd rather call you what your mother calls you."

He smiles. "Well, thank you, Genevieve."

"People try to pull that mess with me, and I make them say it until they get it right. Call me what makes me feel respected, or don't call me anything at all," I say firmly.

"Wow, Genevieve. I've never thought about it that way."

"Being a woman in the military, you get tried all the time. It's like the men are taught not to take women in uniform seriously. They learned very quickly that I wasn't playing about my respect and I learned just as quickly that those jokes' aren't really jokes. I put a stop to it before it could start. Now you, on the other hand, may call me Gigi. I would actually prefer it."

"It's so very nice to meet you, Gigi. I haven't known you five minutes, but I can already tell you're a breath of fresh air," he says, blushing.

"So Olufemi, does your name have a meaning? It's so beautiful."

"Yes, it does. It translates to God loves me.'"

He sure does. He took His time with you.

"You don't say. That's awesome," I chirp as I glance at my watch. 1:39 p.m. "Olufemi, I would love to sit here and talk to you more, but unfortunately, I have to run. I've got to show a house in twenty minutes."

Grabbing my hand he asks, "May I call you sometime, Gigi? I would love to share time with such a beautiful woman. I want to get to know you better."

"Sure, but before I give you my number, can I ask you a few questions?"

"Sure," he retorts.

"Are you married? Do you have children? Do you have a girlfriend? A boyfriend? Are you seeing anyone or is anyone seeing you? Are you a crackhead or functioning alcoholic? Do you do any drugs of any kind, prescribed or not? Do you believe in God? Do you have any diseases, and may I see the paperwork? Are you batshit crazy? A stalker? Does anyone have any injunctions or restraining orders against you? Do you listen to those shitty men's podcasts bashing black women? Did you follow Kevin Samuels before he passed? Are you familiar with Dr. Umar? Do you bunnyhop? Are you a fifty-fifty man? Do I have to bring something to the table? Have you been diagnosed with any mental disorders? And last but not least, are you gainfully employed?"

The thing is, I don't have time to sit here and listen to the answers. Here's my number." I hand him my card.

"Please respond via text when you find the time, okay? Ciao."

He bursts out laughing, takes the card and the check from my hand, and pays for my meal.

"Talk to you soon, Gigi," he says as I saunter out of the bistro.

TIME IS RUNNING OUT, so I whip this Benz, swerving in and out of traffic, trying to get back to the house. I make it with one minute to spare. As I pull up, I see a little dog running around in the front yard. I hop out, and the dog comes running up to me.

"Sheba?? Sheba, is that you?" I whisper, as she jumps at my ankles. I pick her up, and she's so excited that she's practically foaming at the mouth.

What the fuck is going on here?

"Sheba, get down! Get off Miss Parker!" Giselle yells. "I'm so very sorry about that. She's old, but she has lots of energy. She gets a little excited when she meets new people."

"It's okay," I reply, stunned. I can't believe this woman has my dog.

"Oh honey, there he is," she says as a man walks from around the side of the house. "Mrs. Parker, this is my fiancé, Echo."

Chapter Twenty-Five

The minute I lay eyes on him, every ounce of love I'd buried comes rushing back all at once. I want to say something, but I'm too stunned to speak. It's like my brain glitches.

Normally, I'd extend my hand for a handshake, but instead, off impulse, I run in for a hug. He embraces me, and I melt. Just like I did the first time.

"See, honey, I'm not the only one who's a hugger," she says cheerfully.

"Apparently not, Giselle," he mutters, looking me up and down.

"Umm, hi Miss Parker. My name is Echo, as Giselle told you, and it's nice to meet you."

Meet me!?!? Nigga, me? This is business, so I keep it cool.

Cutting my eyes at him, I say, "It's nice to meet you as well, Echo." I begin walking to the front door, and Sheba's right at my heels again. I want to turn around and scoop her up, hug and kiss her, but I resist. I'm not trying to make this more awkward than it already is. I also want to do the same to Echo, but of course, I refrain.

"Sheba sure does like you," Giselle quips.

And I love your fiancé and want to jump his bones, have his kids, and live happily ever after. And of course she likes me. She's MY fucking dog!!!

I open the door, and before I can open my mouth, she grabs Echo's hand and takes off. Apparently, I'm not needed at this moment. Homegirl is doing my job for me, and I don't say a word.

Still in shock, I muster up enough courage to tell them, "If you need me, I'll be in my car. Just signal, and I'll come back in."

I practically run to the Benz while they're upstairs, trying to pull myself together.

What in the fuck is going on here? This can't be happening. This town is too fucking small because what are the chances? My God, Echo is still so fine. And a millionaire. A fucking millionaire?! You mean to tell me this nigga is a millionaire and is about to marry this Pop-Tart?

The millionaire part doesn't surprise me; he's always

had hustle and drive. But the Pop-Tart? That blows me. What the hell does he even see in her?

Given how eager she was about this house, I bet she has him inspecting every corner, just like she did me. They're taking forever, which isn't a bad thing, because I need time to calm down.

I almost never need my meds, but I'm digging in my purse like my life depends on it. I pull one out, place it under my tongue so it works faster.

The last thing I need is to have a mental breakdown in front of this man and his fiancée. I try to talk myself down, deep breaths, calm heart. But when I check my pulse, it's at least 110 bpm. I feel like I just ran three miles.

So much for relaxing.

This is weird as hell. Seeing the love of my life after ten years at a showing was definitely not on my bingo card for today.

Finally, after about an hour, I convince myself to act normal. Especially since this man is pretending not to know me. The last thing I'm about to do is pine over someone who isn't studying me.

But damn, he's still fine as fuck and he has the nerve to be wearing my favorite color shirt, pink.

I reach down and feel the wetness between my legs. A puddle starts to collect in my seat. Thank goodness I brought my blazer.

It's a shame. After all these years, he still makes my pussy drip at the sight of him. He can front if he wants to, but I know he's thinking about me, about us. About all the good times. How could he not? They were too special to forget.

While I'm reminiscing, Ms. Baptiste appears at the front door, motioning for me to come back inside. Her shit-eating grin is gone. I guess he didn't like the house and I don't blame him. It's too old-fashioned for Echo. He's a modern contemporary kind of guy. If she knew him like I did, she would've known that.

I throw on my blazer and trek up the porch to find her standing alone. Within seconds, Echo appears.

"I'm sorry for wasting your time, Gigi," he says. "But we're going to have to pass."

"Gigi? How the fuck do you know that her name is Gigi? I told you her name is Ms. Parker," Ms. Baptiste snaps, looking at him wide-eyed. "Do you two know each other?"

"Umm... yes, Giselle. We do. Sheba originally belonged to her. Ms. Parker and I were a thing back in the day, but I'm sure she's moved on since then. You don't have anything to be concerned about. That was a long time ago." He lowers his head as the words leave his mouth.

"Well, shit, Echo, why didn't you just say that? You didn't have to front for me, baby. You can keep it real. I know your fine tail had a life before me. Whatever happened before me doesn't matter," she says, giving me a long look and grabbing his arm.

"I'm sorry, Ms. Parker, for my reaction. I was just surprised he knew your first name. I'm certain I only told him Ms. Parker.'"

"It's okay, Ms. Baptiste. No offense taken," I say, glancing at Echo.

"Well, I guess it's a no-go on this house then. You were so kind and polite to me that I was going to ask you to be our real estate agent and help us find a house to my fiancé's liking, but seeing that you all have a past, I think it would be a conflict of interest."

"I agree. But I'd be happy to recommend another realtor for you two. I'm sure we can get you into your dream home since Mr. Black doesn't care for this one."

"That sounds great. Can you please text me the name of one of your colleagues, and we'll go from there?"

"No problem. I'll get on that ASAP. I just need to compare schedules, and I'll send that right over," I say as we exit the front door.

I shake both their hands and sashay to my car, hoping Echo's watching so he remembers what he had, and sees what he's missing. I wave goodbye and let them leave first.

Once they're out of sight, I breathe a sigh of relief and return to my Airbnb. The movers are coming in a couple days, so I get busy packing...mostly clothes, shoes, and purses.

While I'm putting my things away, I get a text from an unknown number.

Unknown number: I'd love to answer any questions you have but I'd like to do it over dinner. Can I take you out? Text me back and let me know.

Me: The answers to those questions determine if dinner is even possible. Get to writing, Mr. Olufemi 😌

Unknown number: Duly noted. I'm on it.

Me: Thank you kindly. I await your response.

Just as I'm texting back, I get a call from another unknown number.

I answer. "Olufemi, why would you call me? All you had to do was answer the questions. It can't be that hard."

"Who the hell is an Olufemi, and what questions are you asking him?"

Chapter Twenty-Six

"Now why would you call my phone starting shit, Echo? Especially after you acted like you didn't know me today. Do you know how tight I was? And how did you get this number?"

"Gigi, I'm so sorry for that. I legit almost pissed myself when I saw your face. I didn't know what to say. When did you get back in town and why didn't you let me know?"

"I didn't know I was supposed to. But now that I know you're engaged, I'm glad I didn't go searching for you. I would've been pissed."

"Why would you be pissed? I know you got a nigga somewhere. You're too beautiful not to."

"You may be right about a lot, but you're wrong there. I'm single as a one-dollar bill. You can't say the same. So why are you calling me?"

"Because I wanted to talk to you, Gigi. Girl, I missed the fuck out of you. Can we go out somewhere and catch up? What are you doing right now?"

"I don't deal with men who have significant others. And I can't. I'm packing up to move into my new home."

"Okay then, what's the address? I'll come help. Don't act like you don't need it. I bet you've got tons of shit to move."

"I do... but I'm not sure I can trust you."

"Now you really just hurt my feelings. You know you can trust me. I'd never hurt you. I never have."

"Are you serious right now? Do you realize how much it hurt when you stopped calling me? When you stopped answering my calls? When you stopped writing me back? That hurt the fuck out of me, Echo. You were all I had, and you knew that. It's cool though. I'm over it. I went to therapy like I said I would, and I added you to the list of traumas I needed to release."

"Oh, I'm trauma now?"

"You were. Not anymore. I've worked through that. I'm good now."

"Can I please come over and see you? Please. You know I won't do anything stupid. I just want to spend a little time with you."

"I'm sorry, Echo. You have someone and it's clear she loves you. You asked her to marry you, so I'm assuming you love her just the same. I don't want to interfere. I don't want any smoke."

"Please. Just five minutes of your time. Let me apologize in person. I promise you won't have to be bothered with me again. Let me make this right. I can hear it in your voice. I hurt you and that was never my intention."

"It's 6546 Marley Street. You've got five minutes. And don't try any funny shit. I don't fuck with bear mace anymore. It's Blickyana now."

He laughs. "Thank you, Lil Thugger. I'll see you in twenty."

I experience instant regret the minute my address rolled off my lips. Why in the hell did I tell him where I live? I don't know if I have the sheer willpower not to fuck him raw the minute he walks through the door. I just have to remember...he's no longer mine. And if he were, I wouldn't want someone doing that to me.

I'm going to be on my best behavior and so is he.

Time for a pep talk.

"Gigi, you will not touch him. You will not kiss him. And you definitely will not give him any of your sweet honey pot. Even though you've been wondering since you saw him what that dick do, you are under no circumstances to find out. Okay?"

"Okay," I say to myself, answering my own madness.

I hope no one's watching me through the window. They'd for sure think I was batshit crazy.

As I continue sorting through clothes, I hear a knock at the door. I start walking over, then realize, I'm naked. I sprint back to my room, throw on my robe, and rush to open it.

Standing there is Echo, holding two dozen pink and red roses in one hand and Sheba in the other.

Chapter Twenty-Seven

I grab Sheba and turn around without a word, heading inside.

"Well damn, I'm just chopped liver, huh?" he chuckles.

"You sure are when it comes to this sweet face," I coo, rubbing Sheba's belly. "Do you know how much I've missed you? You're still so adorable. Do me a favor, Sheba. Your real mama needs you to go home and bite the shit outta your step mama's ankles."

I chuckle. "Just kidding. Now that I'm back in town, can I get joint custody? I mean, I *am* her rightful owner."

"Only if you let me bring her to you."

"Why? So you can sniff this sweet pussy and try to fuck on me? I saw the way you looked me up and down at the house. You think you're slick. I'm not about to let you weasel your way back into my heart or my draws."

"Who said anything about draws? You don't hardly wear them anyway."

"Boy, shut up! Don't be telling Sheba my business."

"Where does your old lady think you are? Because I know she doesn't know you're over here. She damn near had a coronary when she heard my name. I'd be careful with that one if I were you. She's probably got a tracker on your ass."

"She's at hot yoga. She's not worried about me."

"Oh, you got a yoga chick, huh? Does she light sage in your house and charge her crystals in the moonlight?" I tease. "Let me guess, she's spiritual, right?"

"Why are you trying to be funny, Gigi? She's an herbalist. And yeah, she burns sage sometimes to clear the negative energy or so she says. We don't live together, so I don't know if she charges her crystals or whatever. How'd you know she considers herself spiritual?"

"She just *seems* like one of those "woke" chicks. No shade, Echo. I'm just saying. I assume from her last name she's probably Creole? That alone tells me a lot. You've seen *Harlem Nights*."

"Come on now. What does her last name have to do with anything? I mean, yeah, she weirds me out sometimes, but only because I didn't know anything about that lifestyle. She's into nature and talking to her ancestors. Hugging trees and shit."

"Oh yeah. Keep her ass away from me with all that. She probably got roots on you or has your ass in a jar somewhere. Shiddd, I'm about to start praying for you now," I say as I fold a dress and pick Sheba back up. "Echo, where's your Bible? I *know* you have one."

"It's at home on my nightstand."

"Good. When you get home, I want you to open it and leave it on your entry table. Turn to Psalm 91 and keep it open at all times."

He laughs. "Ain't no need for all that so you can relax. Giselle's not like that. Yeah, she's from Louisiana, but she doesn't get down like that."

"That's what *you* think," I quip. "But whatever. And there's always a need for God, so I'm gonna pray for you anyway."

"I wasn't talking about not needing God. Of course I need him. I'm saying you don't have to pray like she put roots on me. Like I said, she's not on that."

"Whatever you say," I shrug. Bending over to put Sheba down, my robe betrays me and comes undone. Suddenly my breast and freshly waxed pussy are on full display. Apparently, I don't close it fast enough.

"*Gyaaaattt damn*, Gigi," he groans. "I saw that chocolatey nipple. Please let me suck it. Just one lick."

I glance over. His dick is swelling by the second.

"Girl, why the fuck would you do that to me? I'm about to go crazy. Please let me make love to you. For old time's sake," he pleads.

"Echo, didn't you come over here to *say* something? Get to talking. Your time's almost up."

"I'm sorry. My words escape me. I can't focus. I just saw your nipples and that juicy, plump, smooth pussy and I lost my train of thought. Just let me lick it. Suck it. Shit, just let me *look* at it. Something, Gigi! I'm about to bust. Look at what you do to me!"

He glides his hand over his now huge dick print. "Come on, just the tip. Let my dick smell the pussy, Gigi."

I burst out laughing and do my best to ignore him, even though I clearly see his dick throbbing through his pants. The truth is, I'm salivating from my mouth and pussy. I want him too. But I keep it cute.

"Echo, stop. You didn't come here for this and you can quit rubbing your dick. I'm not doing shit with you. I watched my mother destroy family after family pulling shit like that. I'm not continuing that legacy. I'm not fucking somebody else's man. I'm worthy of my own."

"You damn sure are, Gigi. I'm sorry for acting like this. Please forgive me. But damn...you are so sexy. Even more beautiful than I remember. I told you nobody compares to you. Nobody ever will."

"So why'd you ask her to marry you if that's the case?"

"I didn't. She proposed to me."

"You have got to be fucking kidding me." I suck my teeth.

"I bullshit you not. She got down on one knee and everything, with a ring, in front of her whole family. I figured anyone who'd do that must really love me."

"Or really love your money. But hey, don't listen to me. I don't know shit."

He laughs, then softens.

"While you over there playing, Gigi, I know one thing, that fire between you and me is still burning. It'll never go out."

"Well, it's gonna have to stay smothered for now. You belong to someone else, and I'm not getting in the way. If you ever figure out a way to remedy that problem, call me. Until then, we're just friends."

"I'll take that. I'll take whatever you're willing to give just so I can see you from time to time."

"How long have y'all been together, and when's the wedding?" I ask with a smirk.

"Two and a half years. We haven't set a date. We got engaged three months ago."

"And you're already about to buy her a $4 million house? She must got some mean kitty on her."

"Girl, four million ain't shit to me. Anyway, enough about Giselle. I really came over to tell you I'm sorry for ghosting you like that. I should've been more mature and told you the truth. I couldn't handle being away from you. It wasn't that I didn't want to talk, I did. I missed you so much. But I needed you here. It was like... either I needed all of you, or none of you. I hope you understand. And I hope you forgive me. I never stopped loving you. I never will."

"Thank you for your apology, Echo. It means a lot."

"Damn. I'm surprised you accepted it that easily. Therapy must've really helped. Did it also help with your mom?"

"I wish I could say yes but I haven't spoken to her. She's in a nursing home. I ran into Tasia at a bar. That's how I found out. I went to visit her, but I couldn't go in. I stood outside her door, but my feet wouldn't move. I ran out crying, feeling defeated. I want to try again, but I just don't know, Echo."

"If it'll help, I'll go with you. I know you act all tough and shit, but you still need a support system. Let me be that. My mom loved you. If she knew you were back in town, she'd want to see and support you too. She used to say she could see the sadness in your eyes. Even when you looked happy, she saw through it. She never told me what she knew, but I know my dad told her what he told me.

She genuinely cared for you because she saw how much you loved me."

"Yeah, your mama's a sweetheart. Maybe I'll go see Mrs. Black one day. Hopefully, it won't cause any drama with your old lady."

"No chance. Giselle doesn't go over there. My mom doesn't like her. Says she's "peculiar."

"Mama knows best," I say, laughing.

"Do you still...?" he asks.

"Do I still *what*, Echo?"

"Love me?" he says softly, standing there, desperate for an answer.

Before I can respond, his phone rings.

"Uh-oh. There she is," I tease. "You gonna answer it?"

"Nope," he chirps. "I'll call her on the way home. I don't feel like arguing."

"You still at the townhouse?"

"Yeah, why? You coming back to visit?"

"Hell no. I'm not dumb enough to roll up to somebody else's man's house. That bitch won't get the chance to shoot me dead and get away scot-free."

"It's *my* house. I bought it and I told you we don't live together. You acting like you don't believe me."

"You mean to tell me you didn't meet her and move her in like you did me?" I smirk.

"She's not you. She'll never be you. Now let me get my

ass outta here. Make sure you put those roses in water. And when you're ready to visit your mom, call me. I want to go with you."

"I plan on going soon. I'll text you. I saved your number," I say with a wink.

"Bye, beautiful," he says as he walks out.

Ump, ump, ump. Lord, he is *still* so damn fine to me. Little does he know, I'm using every ounce of restraint I have to keep my legs closed. I honestly don't know how much longer I can resist. Maybe we're better off staying away from each other... because I still love him. And I don't see that changing anytime soon.

Dammit. I wish I never saw him."

Chapter Twenty-Eight

Waking up, I'm a little stressed this morning because I've got a full day ahead of me. Not only do I have five houses to show, but once I'm done, I have to get back to my Airbnb and finish packing before the movers arrive. I should've taken Echo up on his offer to help, but the chemistry between us would've gotten in the way. It's hard as hell to focus on anything when he's around me.

I wonder if Olufemi will help. Nope, let me toss that thought to the side immediately, because I don't know that man well enough to invite him to my home. He could be a complete psycho wrapped in beautiful skin, pretty teeth, and amazing style. I'll just pack all this shit myself. It might take me all night, but I'm gonna get it done.

Grabbing my phone, I unlock it and go straight to my

emails. No one has any special requests, so this day should go smoothly. Going to my messages, I notice Olufemi has responded to my questions.

Olufemi: Good morning, Miss Gigi. I stayed up all night wondering whether I should respond to your questions. Some of them were quite odd, but I decided to answer anyway because there are indeed some nuts around here, but I can assure you I'm not one of them.

Olufemi: I want you to feel completely safe with me. I don't remember every single thing you asked because I didn't have a notepad on hand, but I do remember some, so let me start with the basics:

Olufemi: I'm not crazy. I don't take any kind of medicines or drugs.

Olufemi: I'm healthy as an ox.

Olufemi: I'm not abusive, nor am I a stalker.

Olufemi: I am single. I do not have a girlfriend, and I am not interested in men in any stretch of the imagination.

Olufemi: I've never been married. I don't have any children.

Olufemi: I believe in God; He is the head of my life.

Olufemi: I do not have any diseases and I have the paperwork to prove it.

Olufemi: I don't watch much television; my work doesn't allow much time for anything else.

Olufemi: I don't know who Kevin is, and I've never listened to a podcast.

Olufemi: I love my black queens and I've never been with any other race.

Olufemi: I am gainfully employed as a forensic detective for the city of Roseville.

Olufemi: The only thing my woman needs to bring to the table is the ability to see what the table is missing. That way, she can tell me what we need, and I can go out and get it.

Olufemi: Umm... that's really all I can remember. Hopefully, it'll suffice. If not, I'll be sure to answer anything else on our first date.

HE SOUNDS PRETTY normal to me. One date won't hurt. If it doesn't work out, I'll go on with my life and so will he. I guess I'll give him a shot.

Me: Thank you so much for taking the time to answer my questions. You're right, there are some nuts out there, and that's the reason I try to vet everyone I let into my life.

Me: Anyway, dinner sounds great, but it can't be tonight. I've got some business to handle. But I definitely want to take a rain check. I'll reach back out to you when I'm ready. How does that sound?

Olufemi: Sounds great. Hope to hear from you soon. Have a great day.

STILL LYING IN BED, I glance at the clock. It reads 6:26 AM. I hop out of bed and make my way to the kitchen to make a strong pot of coffee to get me going. I put in an extra scoop for good measure. I need that extra boost today. While the coffee brews, I take a shower, pick out my clothes, and get dressed.

As I walk back to the kitchen, the doorbell rings.

No one knows where I 'm staying, and I'm not

expecting visitors, so I run back to my room to grab Blickyana.

Quietly, I walk to the front door. It rings again. Lowering my gun behind my back, I crack the door to find Mrs. Baptiste standing on my porch.

Opening the door wider, I buck my eyes at her because what in the fuck is she doing here? And this early in the morning, no less?

"Can I help you?"

"Yes, Miss Business Suit, you can! This address showed up on Echo's location last night, and I just wanted to come by and see who lived here. You wanna tell me why my man was at this motherfucking house last night?"

"Hold on, Giselle, I know th—"

"It's *Ms.* Baptiste, *soon-to-be Mrs. Black* to you," she snaps, cutting me off mid-sentence.

"Ms. Baptiste, I think that's a question you should ask Echo. I don't want to get involved in whatever you two have going on. Plus, I can assure you that whatever you think it is, it isn't."

"You got involved the second you let him come over here. I don't play that kind of shit. Ain't no nigga or prissy-ass bitch about to play in my face. I think you slid him your address when I wasn't looking, and I don't appreciate thirsty bitches like you coming after my man.

You need to realize that whatever it was you two had is in the past, and that's where the fuck it's gonna stay!!"

My hand is still tucked behind my back, and I lower it slowly so she can see exactly what she's dealing with.

"That is the *last* bitch I'll be today. I tried to be nice, but I see you want to be ignorant so I'm going to be ignorant right along with you.

Get the fuck off my porch before you leave this bitch leaking," I advise through gritted teeth. "I'm not going to ask you again and you might want to think twice about rolling up on someone else's property. They might not be as nice as me."

"Yeah, whatever, prissy bitch. I've got something for that ass."

"Uh-huh, whatever. Go on and hop back on your broomstick and get the fuck on. And please, *have the day you deserve you crazy bitch*," I say, slamming the front door and locking it behind me.

Chapter Twenty-Nine

See? I told Echo that bitch was crazy. This is *exactly* why I don't deal with other women's men. Comes with too many problems. Some of these chicks be ready to die about a dick. I pray I'm never that pressed.

Running back to my bedroom, I grab my phone off the nightstand and dial Echo's number immediately.

"Well good morning, beautiful. I must've done something right last night for you to be calling me this early."

"No, nigga. You're getting this phone call because your bitch just rolled up on my porch like she was Nino Brown or somebody. She almost got her ass popped! What the fuck is wrong with you, Echo? If you knew you were coming over here, why wouldn't you turn your location off?"

"Location? What are you talking about, Gigi? I don't share my location with her... at least I don't think I do. Hold on, let me check that shit right now.

I guess I do. She must've taken my phone and shared my location to hers. I didn't even know. I'm sorry about that. I'll handle her."

"You better or *I* will. She won't get another chance to call me another bitch again. You know I've got a thing about people talking to me crazy."

"I know, baby, and I'm sorry."

He completely throws me off my shit when that word rolled off his lips.

"Baby." I used to love when he called me that. Damn. He doesn't even know it, but he still makes me weak... and makes me leak.

"It's cool," I say, trying not to let on how that word has me feeling. "It's not your fault that she's batshit crazy, but I *did* tell you to watch yourself and I meant it. Now, maybe you understand why."

"Let me go. I've got to get my day started. I've got so much to do. I'll talk to you later."

"Wait, Gigi... were you serious about us being friends? Like, the kind of friends that go out and do things together? Or the kind of friends who see each other in passing and wave?"

"What are you trying to get to, Echo?"

He pauses before speaking.

"There's a car show I want to check out next weekend. I'm looking to cop a few new rides for my collection. You want to come with me?"

"That sounds like fun, Echo, but I'm going to have to decline. With your guard dog rolling up on me and me moving into my new home, I just won't have the time. But I hope your trip won't be in vain. I hope you find the baddest rides out there."

"Thanks," he says in a tone full of sadness.

I can tell he feels let down, but I can't make that my problem. I've got too much to do.

"Bye, Echo."

"Later, Sweetheart and again, I'm sorry."

I pour my coffee and drink it at light speed as I stare at the boxes on the floor. I begin sifting through them in search of my gun holster. This way, I can keep Blickyana on me and not in my purse. He couldn't have told her shit about me, because if he had, she wouldn't have brought that nonsense to my doorstep. Strapping up, I grab my keys, my purse, and I'm out the door. That crazy bitch won't catch me slipping. I'm on high alert from now on.

Peeping the scene while walking to my car, I notice a $100 bill in the driveway. As I walk over to it, something stops me dead in my tracks and tells me not to touch that shit. I back away, hop in my car, and drive off. I'm not scared of anything on this earth with two legs, but I have to admit, this is some weird shit.

I don't like to have my peace disturbed under any circumstances, and that's exactly what this situation has done. Now I'm even more worried for Echo than I was before. I'm praying that he takes heed to my warnings and doesn't take them as a joke.

Looking into her eyes earlier was like staring into the abyss. Nothing was there. Maybe I'm reading more into it than I should, but I don't trust a soul.

As busy as my day is, I don't have the mental capacity to worry about her. I try to go about my day as normal, showing house after house and drawing up paperwork in between each viewing.

Driving back to the office, I receive a phone call from my coworker Angel, letting me know that a delivery is waiting for me. Thanking her for the heads-up, I swerve in and out of traffic until I pull into the office parking lot.

I hop out my ride and saunter into the building to find four dozen pink and red roses on my desk.

Angel is just a few steps behind me, smiling like a maniac. I ignore her with every step.

"Girl, why are you walking so close to me? What does your nosy ass want?"

"I'm waiting for you to open the card so we can see who they're from! Shit, you just got back in town and you've already made a love connection. I'm jealous. I've been here all my life and still haven't managed that. What's your secret?"

"There is no secret, Angel. I don't even have to look at the card to know who they're from. They're from my ex-boyfriend. He knows pink is my favorite color, and red means love, so he always mixes the two."

"That's so sweet, girl. Y'all must've had one hell of a love connection. He's still buying you roses after all this time? He must've been the first person you called when you got back to Roseville."

"Not at all. We reunited by happenstance. You know that house on Forester, the huge traditional one that's been on the market forever?The one we can't get rid of?"

"Yes, I know exactly the house you're talking about." Angel says as she leans in to get the tea.

"Well she's the one that called about it and wanted to look at it. You sent me the email about her the other day."

"I remember...the one you told you couldn't show the house that day, but said you'd show it the next day?"

"Yep, that's her. Anyway, she shows up to the viewing with my ex, and I play it cool. No weird shit between us, strictly business. He made the mistake of calling me by my first name and she went off. I was cool with that, because hey, the brother is gorgeous, and it's easy to think everyone wants your man when he's that fine. But that wasn't the case. I wasn't studying him like that.

Well, after the showing, he gets my number from the business card and calls to apologize to me for some things he did in the past. I let him come over, not thinking anything of it because I knew what my intentions were. And tell me why this morning, his crazy-ass girlfriend shows up on the porch at my Airbnb."

Chapter Thirty

"Oh my God, are you serious? That's scary!" Angel announces.

"Yeah. Something's not right about her, and I tried to tell him, but he thinks it's a game."

"Girl, I've been here all my life. What's her name? I probably know her."

"I've been here most of my life too, and I don't recognize her at all. He says she's from Louisiana. I don't know much about her because I didn't ask, but I know she needs to tread lightly when it comes to me. Her name is Giselle Baptiste."

"Gigi, my brother is a police officer. I can have him run a check for you if you want me to."

"No, it's not necessary. I'm good, Angel but thank you

anyway," I say, grabbing the card from the bouquet of flowers.

I know I've already apologized, but I felt like I needed to do it again. I'm sorry for dragging you into this bullshit, but I told her not to ever fuck with you or come near you again. I just hope her crazy ass listens.

Love you always,

Echo.

Smiling, I lower the card into my purse and sit down to start on my paperwork. By the time I'm done, it's almost pitch-black outside. I hate daylight savings time. It gets dark too early for me.

I pack up my things, set the alarm, and head out the door. Once I reach the parking lot, I notice that my front driver-side tire is flat.

Ain't this 'bout a bitch.

I look around, and no one is in sight but I *feel* like I'm not alone.

I head back into the building and call Olufemi to see if he can come help me change the tire. My first instinct was to call Echo, but with everything going on, I didn't think that would be a good idea.

Olufemi doesn't answer, so I end up calling Echo anyway.

He picks up on the first ring.

"Are you busy?"

"Not busy enough to keep me from talking to you. What's up?"

"I kind of need your help. I didn't want to call you, but I didn't have anyone else to call."

"You know I got you. What do you need?"

"I just got off work, went to get in my car, and realized that my front tire is flat. Can you come help me fix it, please?"

"Sure. Drop your pin. I'm on the way."

While waiting for him to arrive, I flip on the lights to make sure the place is fully illuminated, then close all the blinds. I could've sworn I saw a shadow pass by the window, but maybe I'm trippin. This whole situation has me on edge, and I don't like it.

Within minutes, he pulls into the parking lot with a damn flatbed trailer. He is so extra. I asked him to change a tire, and he shows up ready to haul the entire car. Like, just change the tire so I can go home. I don't want to seem ungrateful, but I'm pressed for time. Plus, I can't help but feel like his old lady had something to do with this mess.

"Sir, what do you have going on? Why do I feel like you're trying to get me somewhere so I'm on *your* turf?"

"Girl, you suspicious of everybody but you do know me pretty well," he says, smirking. "I just wanna take it to my shop to make sure everything's good with it."

"Let me ask you something, Echo. Where was Giselle between three and five? Do you know?"

"No, Gigi, I don't. She stopped by the house this afternoon and said she had some errands to run. I haven't seen her since."

"I *bet* you haven't."

"You trying to say you think she did this?"

"I don't know who did what, but all this weird shit has been happening ever since I met her. Not to mention the hundred-dollar bill that miraculously showed up in my driveway this morning after her ass left."

"Enough about her," Echo urges. "Hop in while I get this thing on the flatbed, and then we'll go handle this real quick."

He must do this kind of thing often because it takes him literally five minutes to get the car loaded. We hit the interstate, heading God knows where but I have to admit, I may not trust a lot of people, but I *do* trust him.

Within fifteen minutes, we arrive at a top-of-the-line mechanic shop and garage. He tells me to go inside while he handles the car.

Inside, I look around at all his accomplishments. My boy is *goated* in the car game. There are so many trophies, I can't even begin to count them. On the wall, I see pictures of Mr. and Mrs. Black, his grandfather, and some of the most famous entertainers you could think of. Then I come across a picture of an 18-year-old me, standing next to the Maxima, and I almost pass out.

I can't believe he still has this photo and it's on his wall *with family*, no less. My heart warms, and I feel all fuzzy and tingly inside. I guess my heart isn't cold and dead after all.

At last, she *feels* again.

Chapter Thirty-One

"Gigi, your tire was slashed, and the other three had tiny holes in them that would've caused a slow leak," he tells me. "Don't worry, I'll order four new tires and have them put on as soon as they arrive."

"Echo, I truly don't have time for all of this. So now I have to go get a rental until this is done? Today is just my lucky fucking day, isn't it?" I exhale sharply. "I know one thing, you better keep that bitch away from me, because I know she did this. Who else would've done it? I've only been back in this town a minute and I'm already regretting my decision."

"Don't say that, Gigi. If you only knew how happy I am that you're back. Even if we aren't together, just being able to see your face every now and again, makes me happy as shit."

"I wish I could feel that same joy, but right now all I feel is pissed. I'm gonna be cool, though. I didn't spend all that money on therapy for nothing. Can you take me to a car rental place so I can go handle this?"

"No, I won't. Look around. Do you not see all these cars? Pick one."

"I'm not doing that. You paying for and ordering new tires for me is already too much. As soon as they come in, I want you to tell me the cost so I can reimburse you."

"And you know damn well I'm not gonna let you do that. Learn how to accept kindness. Your therapist may have worked with you on a lot of shit, but obviously, that part was left out. You still don't like accepting help from anyone. You're as stubborn as a damn mule."

"Whatever you say, Echo. Just give me the keys to one of these cars so I can get back to my place and finish what I have to do. Tomorrow, the movers get here and I'm out of the Airbnb and into my own shit. I can't wait."

"So you bought a house, huh? When do I get to see it?"

"No time soon, sir. I want you to keep all this drama on this side of town. Don't bring that shit to mine."

"Don't worry, I won't. And if Giselle had anything to do with this, just know it's over between us. I mean done."

"You'd really break up with her over this?"

"Hell yeah. In a heartbeat. I don't do well with this type of messy shit. You've been through enough. I'm not about to let somebody come in and fuck up all the progress you've made. I don't know what I'd do if something happened to you. Shit, I just got you back and I'm not about to let you go. I'll let her ass go though."

I burst out laughing.

"Here you go. Enjoy." Tossing me the keys to a navy blue 1971 Monte Carlo. A real classic and I can't front, the car is beautiful and completely restored.

Catching the keys, I unlock the door and get in. The inside is *sick*. Wood grain, bucket seats, the whole nine.

"Will you call me when my car is done so I can come pick it up?"

"Would you rather me do that or bring it to you, since you'll be busy?"

"Yes, that's fine. Actually, that would help me a lot, so thank you. Thank you for everything."

"You know you don't have to thank me but you're welcome. And don't worry, I'm gonna get to the bottom of this shit. I know Giselle is a little touched. I like my women a little crazy, but not *this* kind of crazy. I can't rock with no chick doing shit like this. Busting windows and flattening tires is the kind of shit kids do. We're supposed to be grown, and I've got too much to lose."

"You and me both," I yell, while backing out of the garage.

He blows a kiss and waves goodbye.

I merge onto the interstate and push this bitch to the floor and it doesn't disappoint. I can feel the sheer power in this car, and I feel like I own the road.

Now I completely understand why he loves what he does. Seeing his warehouse makes me so proud. He's done so well for himself and nothing turns me on more than a man who keeps his word and goes after what he wants. He put a plan in action while we were kids and he carried it out in a way that I'd never imagined. He'd always said that he would be someone special and he turned his dreams into a reality. That damn Echo. I can't do anything but shake my head and smile.

Chapter Thirty-Two

Arriving back at my Airbnb, I find the door cracked open and my shit is literally everywhere. It looks like a Tasmanian devil tore through the place. Boxes are open and scattered across the floor, water is running from the sink and has soaked the kitchen, dining room, and part of the living room. Glass is shattered all over the floor and countertops. The place has been completely vandalized, and the letters *H I M A W A B M S* are spray-painted on the walls of every single room. I don't know what it means and at this point, I don't care. I just want all of this to go away.

Standing in the middle of the chaos, I try to calm myself by doing my breathing exercises, but it feels like there isn't enough oxygen on this damn earth to bring me down.

Reaching into my purse, I pull out my pills and pop one. I'm so overwhelmed I don't even know where to begin. I guess I should start by calling the police... then the owners of this house. I'm convinced it was her. I haven't done anything to anyone. Hell, I didn't even do anything to her, but perception is reality in some people's world.

I call the police, and they send an officer out immediately, who, coincidentally, turns out to be Angel's brother. I alert the owners of the house and they send a family member over to assess the damage. The police begin gathering evidence and processing the scene, and no one is allowed inside until they finish.

There are officers everywhere. It's proving to be too much for me to handle, so I go sit in the Monte Carlo and Echo scares the shit out of me when he opens the passenger side and hops in.

"What in the hell are you doing here? I was just about to call you," I yelp.

"Well, when you left, something didn't feel right, so I decided to come check on you before I headed back to my house. I'm glad I did. What the hell is going on in there?"

I explain everything in detail, and his mouth is wide open. Without any prompting, he pulls out his phone and calls Giselle, putting her on speaker.

"I'm going to ask you this one time, and one time only."

"Ask me what, baby?" she says, trying to play coy.

"Did you have anything to do with what happened to Gigi's car and house?"

"Listen, that bitch had an attitude and pulled her gun out on me. All I did was ask her if y'all were messing around. Instead of just telling me what I needed to know, she got slick, so I got slicker."

"So the answer is yes?"

"Yes, Echo, but I just needed her to know how I'm coming behind you. Where I'm from, you pull a gun on me and don't use it, then it's game on."

Not being able to take it anymore, I yell, "I did *not* pull a gun on you, you dumbass bitch! I answered the door with the gun *in my hand* and showed it to you as an incentive to get the hell out of my yard! I told you it wasn't anything like that. You took it this far over nothing. Then—"

"Wait, wait...so, Echo, you mean to tell me you're *there* with that bitch right now?" she says, cutting me off mid-sentence. "I just *know* you didn't call me from her crib. Both of y'all have lost y'all motherfucking minds. Do you and that slut know what I'm capable of? It's obvious that you don't."

"Girl, I'm not trying to hear all that. I asked you a question and you gave me an answer. When I get home, I'll be boxing up the little bit of shit you have at my place and having one of my homeboys drop it off wherever you want me to," he barks.

"Echo, are you seriously going to box up my things over this petty shit?" She whines.

"Hell yeah and there is nothing petty about this. This is nuts. I'm just glad I never gave your loco ass a key to my place. You're doing *way* too much, and I don't know what kind of man you think I am, but I am *not* with all this craziness. I already didn't know how to feel about half the weird shit you do, but this? This took the cake. You flattened this girl's tires and basically destroyed her home. And for what? *Nothing.* Nothing is going on between us. Nothing happened. So you messed up with me over some shit you *thought* was happening. No proof, just your craziness and assumptions."

"Yeah, nigga, you're telling me I'm assuming, but you're with that bitch *right now.* Lies don't give a fuck who tells them."

"Giselle, I don't know who hurt you, but it wasn't me. And I *cannot* deal with this kind of shit. So it's over. The engagement is off. Don't ever come near me again, for *anything.* That's on my soul. Stay the fuck away from *us.*"

"*Us*? So y'all together now? Because just a day ago, *we* were us. You was—" *Boop.* He hangs up in her face, blocks her number, and turns to me.

"Sweetness, I don't even know what to say except I'm

sorry for all of this. But that 'problem' you wondered if I could remedy? It's not going to be a problem anymore."

"Are you sure about that? Because something tells me she's not the type to just go away. She's the type of bitch that'll fight to the death over *her* man. I mean, it's obvious. Look how much havoc she's caused in *just one day.*"

"Yes I'm sure, Gigi. I'm telling you. If she comes near me or you again, then it's going to be *her* ass."

Chapter Thirty-Three

As we sit there talking, an officer walks up to the car and asks me to step out.

"Ma'am, we've been in correspondence with the property owners regarding the cameras, and they'll be sending over the footage shortly. Hopefully, it'll show us who did this."

"I already know who did it," I say, motioning for Echo to get out of the car. He does and then sings like a canary.

"I'm sorry, Officer, but my fiancée, well, ex-fiancée did this," Echo explains as he shakes the officer's hand.

"Oh, wow. Did she really confess?" the officer asks, surprised.

"She did, and I recorded the phone call. I'm not sure if it'll help, since I didn't get her permission, but we know she did it and she's proud of it. If there are cameras around the perimeter, they'll show her."

"Can you give us a description of the suspect?"

"Sure," Echo replies eagerly. "She's light-skinned, with long brown and blonde braids that she usually wears in a bun. Petite in stature. She has a septum piercing and a nose ring. Hazel eyes, and a large chakra tattoo on her forearm. I was half asleep when she came by earlier, so I'm not sure what she was wearing."

"I remember," I chime in. "She had on a mustard-colored jogging set with a hoodie and black Air Force Ones."

"Oh, she wears black Air Force Ones... she definitely did it," the officer chuckles.

Echo and I stand there and look at him. Not finding the humor in this shit. He gets the drift, clears his throat and continues, "Umm, thank you both for the descriptions and your cooperation. Ma'am, would you like to press charges?"

"Yes," Echo and I say in unison.

"She would also like to file a restraining order against her," Echo adds. "Not only did she destroy this house, but she also flattened the tires on her brand-new ride. I really hope it stops here. Now that I think about it, I just broke up with her, so I might need to file a restraining or trespassing order too. I don't want her breaking into my shit and trashing my place next."

"We can do all of that," the officer replies, "but I'll need you both to come down to the station so we can gather the necessary information. A judge has to approve any restraining orders."

"Say less," Echo mutters.

The officer, standing there with his little notepad, lets us know they'll need more time to dust the house for fingerprints, take photos of the damage, and review the security footage. Once that's all done, I'll be allowed back inside to see what I can salvage.

An unmarked police car pulls up, and Olufemi hops out, heading towards the house. He spots me out of the corner of his eye, slows his pace and walks directly over.

"What are you doing here, Gigi? Please don't tell me it's your house that been vandalized."

"It's not *my* house, per se, but I'm staying here for now. Wait, what are *you* doing here? I thought you said you were a detective. Shouldn't you be out solving a murder or something?"

He chuckles. "I'm a forensic detective, not homicide. Totally different ballgame. Anyway, who's this guy standing next to you like a bodyguard?"

"My name's Echo, and I can speak for myself. I'm a

good friend of hers. We go way back. Like wayyy, wayyy back. Ya dig?"

"Gigi, do you know him personally?" Echo asks.

"Damn, Echo. Can we not do this? None of this shit matters right now. I've got to figure out where I'm staying tonight and about a dozen other things. I don't have it in me to explain anything to anybody."

"Understood," Olufemi says quietly. "Well, I'm here in a professional capacity, so let me get to it. Hopefully, we'll talk later," he adds, giving Echo a pointed look as he walks away toward the house.

"You know what, Echo? All this is too much. I'm tired, hungry, and pissed off. That bitch destroyed all my expensive shit including the stuff I use for work! My vintage suits, my shoes, crystalware, glassware, cookware... Busted wine bottles. My handbags have spray paint on them! Like, who does that?

And she destroyed these nice people's house. I'm not even tripping about the stuff because I can replace it all three times over if I have to, but that's not the point. It's the principle. I hate being tried.

I'm telling you now, if she runs up on me, I will put her ass down like the dog she is. And I won't think twice about it. I've done far worse in the military. It won't be shit to actually end a bitch who has it out for me."

"Gigi, do you know where you're staying tonight?"

"Not with *you*, if that's what you're thinking. Unless they catch her, that bitch might set the damn house on fire while we're asleep. I'm going to a hotel. And I'm taking tomorrow and the rest of the week off. I need time to get situated.

How could you deal with someone like that, Echo? What were you thinking?" I side-eye the hell out of him while I wait for an answer.

"Gigi, do you really think she'd ever shown me that side of herself before? No. She was sweet as pie...until today."

"Are you seriously going to dump her like that? You know, if I didn't know any better, I'd think you were *looking* for a reason to call off the engagement." I look him in the eyes, searching for the truth. "You seem *real* comfortable letting her go."

Without saying a word, Echo grabs my hand and leads me back to the car. He opens the passenger door and tells me to get in and wait. Then he walks up to one of the officers, hands him a card, says a few words, shakes his hand, and comes back.

"What was all that?" I ask.

"I gave him my card and told him you were hungry, shaken up, and exhausted. I let him know we'll be back later, and if they needed to speak with you before then, they could call me. I'm getting you out of here, away from all this bullshit."

"What about your car?"

"I texted one of my homeboys. He's on his way to pick it up and take it back to the garage. Don't worry about any of this, Gigi. I've got you covered and I'll take care of whatever you need."

Chapter Thirty-Four

"Here you go being you. Coming to my rescue yet again. If you're my guardian angel, just say that."

"If I were your guardian angel, you wouldn't have gone through half the things you've been through. You would've known as a child that you were good enough. You wouldn't have been abused and misused. And you definitely wouldn't have felt the need to join the military just to escape and leave me all alone.

None of that would've happened. So no, I'm not your guardian angel. But I *am* the man who promised that as long as I was around, I wouldn't let anyone or anything hurt you. That you'd be safe with me. That promise hasn't changed. I still mean it."

His words move me to tears as usual. I turn my head

toward the window and silently weep before asking, "Where are we going, Echo?"

"Please, just trust me. Somewhere safe where you and I don't have to worry about Giselle's psycho ass."

"We can't go too far, Echo. I've got to stay close in case they call needing more information." I advise.

"Ain't that what phones are for? Besides, we'll still be in Roseville. Just on the outskirts, so don't worry, Precious."

We hit the backroads, and the car is silent for most of the ride. Unsure of what he's thinking, I break the silence.

"I'm hungry. Can you stop so I can get something to eat?"

"Now you know I'm gonna feed you. If I don't do anything else. Believe it or not, Gigi, I'm the same man I was when you left. Just a little older, a little wiser, and a little richer but I'm still me."

"I know, Echo. I can see and appreciate the growth in both of us. But I'd be lying if I said this whole situation doesn't have me livid. I don't need her finding out where my new house is and doing something to *that*. I'm just hoping those homeowners have insurance to cover the damage she caused. It's sad," I continue. "People work hard for what they have, and she just comes along and destroys it over some bullshit."

"Let's not worry about any of that right now," he mutters.

As we're riding, I get a text message from Olufemi.

Olufemi: Are you OK?

Me: As OK as I'm going to be. Today was shit, but tomorrow will be better. I'm claiming it. Thank you for checking on me.

Olufemi: Of course. I needed to make sure that sweet face of yours is alright. Will I be able to see you sometime soon? Outside of work? lol

Me: We'll see. Hopefully, you catch her ass and throw her in jail for a little bit. That would definitely make my week.

Olufemi: The owner sent over the videos, and the suspect looks exactly like you described...clothes and all. So you've definitely got a case, and she's definitely guilty.

Olufemi: She's got a mean rap sheet too. You need to teach your friend how to vet people like you vetted me because he's obviously too trusting. We're talking stalking, battery, harassment, fraud, assault, burglary, intimidating a witness… the list goes on.

Me: I'll let him know. But I'm telling you now...my .45 doesn't leave my side. If she runs up on me, you're gonna need one of your coworkers from the coroner's office, because it'll be a wrap for her. I don't want to hurt anyone but I'll do what I have to do to protect myself.

Olufemi: Please stay safe out there. I'll catch up with you later.

Me: Will do.

"ECHO, can I ask you a question? And please don't get offended."

"Ohhh shit, what did I do now?"

"I'm just trying to understand how someone like you gets caught up with someone like her. That was the detective from earlier today. He told me Giselle has a rap sheet as long as my arm."

"Gigi, quit playing!"

"I'm serious, Echo. He said she's been arrested for stalking, battery, burglary...I mean, the list goes on. Once we get to wherever we're going, I'll let you read the messages for yourself. So, how did this happen? Where did you meet her?"

"Her dad bought one of my cars for her. She was into vintage vehicles like me. I had a 1977 Dodge Monaco. She was canary yellow and in pristine condition. He brought her with him, and it went from there."

"Oh, I see. Y'all had some things in common to bond over. That makes sense."

"Yeah. But I don't know *that* crazy chick who showed up at your crib. I've never seen her before. That's a different person," he says as we pull onto a dirt road in the middle of nowhere.

"Boy, what is this? Where are you taking me?"

"Somewhere nobody knows about," he smiles, putting me at ease.

After driving for another mile and a half, we arrive at a single log cabin nestled deep in the forest.

Turning to me he mutters, "Gigi, you are getting an exclusive. Not even my parents know this exists. My grandfather and I built it together. We worked all summer when

I was 14. This is the land I told you about when we first met. It's dark now so you can't see, but there's a lake right behind it. The view is beautiful. Come on, get out. Let me show you around."

He walks around to open my car door, and we head to the front porch hand in hand. Normally, I'd be on edge. It's pitch black out here. I can't even see my hand in front of my face. But with his hand wrapped around mine, I feel invincible.

He makes me feel like I can't be fucked with. A mountain lion could charge out right now, and I probably wouldn't even flinch because I know he'd lay down his life to protect me. I've always felt that with him. I've been trained by the best, and I know I can handle myself. But Echo puts me in such a soft-girl space that I don't even worry. He handles it. He *always* has.

He uses his phone's flashlight to find the keyhole. I don't know what to expect but if I know him, the inside is beautiful. Once he opens the door, I realize I was right.

The outside looked like a basic log cabin, but the inside is rustic and chic. Bear rugs cover the floor. Deer heads with massive antlers are mounted on the walls. It's equipped with everything one needs. A refrigerator, gas stove, wood-burning stove, bathroom, and bedroom. It's the perfect getaway for anyone seeking peace.

"Echo, I thought you said you were going to feed me."

"And I am," he says, walking over to the freezer and pulling out two Hungry Man meals.

I scream laughing. He used to keep these stocked for the days I was too tired to cook. His favorite was the Salisbury steak with mashed potatoes and corn and that's exactly what he puts in the microwave.

"Girl, I told you I'd feed you good. You were in the military. If you could eat MREs, your ass can eat a Hungry Man meal."

"I didn't say I wasn't gonna eat it. I'm just tickled you still eat these. Echo, do you know how much sodium is in one of these things?"

"Gigi, I want you to look me in the eyes and tell me if you see *one ounce* of give-a-damn. These things are good and they come through in a clutch."

When the microwave dings, he hands me my meal. I wait for his to finish, and we sit at the small dining table, say grace, and eat. I have to admit, it's delicious. But that might be because I haven't eaten all day. That one cup of coffee was all I had, and I've been on the go ever since.

As we're enjoying our TV dinners, Echo's phone rings. He answers with a mouthful of food and puts it on speaker.

"What's up, Wood?"

"Aye man, where you at?"

"I'm off in the cut. What's up?"

"Man, I need you to get your ass to the shop. This girl's gone *crazy* over here. I was getting ready to lock up when I heard something outside. I go check it out, and it's your old lady with a big-ass gas can, throwing gas around the building. We caught her, and we're holding her here. You want us to call the police?"

"Nope. Keep her right there. I'm on the way."

Chapter Thirty-Five

"Damn, Echo. This girl is really crazy about you. You definitely did that thing you do to her, because ain't no way," I grumble in an exhausted tone. "This shit makes no sense. She's truly a fucking psycho."

"Grab your things, Gigi. We've got to go."

We didn't even get 30 full minutes to rest before we had to book it back into town and deal with this psycho-ass chick. I'm tempted to tell him to just drop me off at a hotel, but curiosity tells me to shut the hell up. I want to see how he handles this.

Within twenty minutes, we're back in town and headed to the shop. He's playing,"2 Slippery by Bossman Dlow," and he is amped as hell. Rapping and spitting everywhere. I'm ticked at him, but also a tad nervous about what's to come.

We hit the curve heading into the shop, seemingly on two wheels. Hopping out, we run into the building.

They've got her tied to a chair with old, greasy mechanic shop towels. Her mouth is gagged with what looks like a dirty sock and duct tape. As soon as we step inside, her eyes widen and she starts going crazy. Rocking the chair, doing everything in her power to get to us. But she's having no luck.

"Aye, Wood, take that shit out of her mouth," he commands. "I need to talk to her and find out what kind of crazy shit she's on."

Wood does as he's told. The moment the sock is removed, she spits in his face. Wood slaps her so hard her jaw rocks and her lips swell instantly.

"Damn, Echo, man. I'm sorry. I didn't mean to hit her like that; it was a reflex."

"Oh, you're good, big fella. She had that one coming."

"Giselle, don't you know that spitting on someone is assault? I'm sure you do, since you've been charged with it before, haven't you?"

"Fuck you, Echo. You let this bitch come back into town and ruin everything for us! We were doing just fine before Miss Business Suit decided to step on my toes!"

Looking at me, she yells, “Bitch, you should’ve stayed where the fuck you were!”

“Giselle, she didn’t do shit. I got the business card and called her, not the other way around. She wasn’t checking for me and probably still wouldn’t be if your ass hadn’t done what you did. And I’m glad you did though. The love of my life is back, and I have *you* to thank for it.”

“See, the thing is, Giselle, I liked you a lot. But as hard as I tried, I could never give you my all. I really did try, but it was like something was blocking me from fully giving myself to you the way I did to her. You’ve got everything a man could want. You’re beautiful, was sweet as pie until today, can cook, can fuck, suck a mean dick, yet something was missing. For the longest time, I didn’t know what it was. Now I do. I was overcomplicating it.”

“It’s simple: you are not for me. You’re not my person. Gigi is and she always has been.”

“Fuck you! That bitch probably just wants you for what you have. Bitches always checking for you 'cause they’re looking for a meal ticket. That’s damn sure what got me.”

I interrupt with, “Girl, please shut the fuck up. You don’t know me or shit about me. I don’t need or want a man to depend on. If you knew me, you’d know that,” I scoff.

Echo chimes in. “Giselle, that’s where you’re wrong.

She was with me when I was still fixing cars in folks' yards. It's never been about what I could do for her. Not with Gigi. This is way deeper than that. What you don't know is that we consulted God about this thing we have. When we were kids, we said if it was meant to be, it would be. And thanks to you... it is. You did exactly what you needed to do to make sure we crossed paths again. It's called Divine timing.

If you didn't want to go see that old ugly, tacky-ass house, I wouldn't have known she was back. If you hadn't gone to her house this morning and almost got your ass shot, she wouldn't have called me to fuss. Even then, she said her piece and got off the phone. But nooooo, you had to keep going.

When you flattened her tires, she called me to help her. By then, it had already clicked. I knew you were on that bullshit and that I was really done."

Then your dumb ass went and broke in and vandalized her house. On camera, I might add. And guess who was there to comfort her, just like I've always done? Me."

I cut in. "Giselle, oh wait, excuse me...*Ms. Baptiste*, the sad thing is, I was willing to push my feelings for Echo aside because of you. I told him I wouldn't deal with a man in a relationship, so he tried to respect my boundaries. Even though we both knew the love we had was still there. I was gonna stay on ice because of you. But you fucked all that up. So, in my opinion, you're getting exactly what you deserve."

"Bitch, shut up. Don't talk to me, you whore. He's my nigga. Period. Point. Blank." Giselle boasts. "Did you not read the writings on the wall. I literally put it in every room in the house. He is my man and will always be my man, slut. I know you were wondering what those letters meant, now you know."

"Giselle, yo ass is really *delulu*. Are you not hearing what I'm saying to you? I. Am. Not. Your. Nigga. If we're being honest, I realized the moment I saw her face at that ugly-ass house that it was over for you. I knew then I could stop fooling myself."

"Don't say those things, Echo. You don't really mean it," she says, visibly agitated. "Seriously, shut up. I don't want to hear this shit," she screams at the top of her lungs. "Fuck you and that bitch. She could never be me. You'll never get over me. You can't. I'll always be with you somehow. I made sure of it."

"You're right. She could never be you and that's the good part. I was gonna try to let you down easy, let things fade off gradually. But you forced my hand. Do you really think it's hard to get over you, Giselle? You're already a thing of the past and don't even know it. There's no way I could stay with anyone who could and would do half the shit you've done and in one day. Girl, you must be part demon, because how can you sleep at night, knowing the shit you've done? Your arrest record is bananas," Echo chuckles.

"Easy, motherfucker. I tuck my pillow behind my head and close my fucking eyes. You're just talking shit 'cause that slut is standing there. If she wasn't in the picture, you'd be eating out my ass right now," Giselle proclaims.

"You know, Giselle—," I chime.

"Don't say my name, you slut!" she growls, cutting me off.

"You know, Giselle," I continue, calm and unfazed, "I told Echo you were on some weird shit, like you probably had him in a jar somewhere. But don't you know all that stuff is no match for God? Girl, I've been praying for this man since I was 17. Day after day, night after night. I prayed that no harm would come to him. I asked that he be protected from both the seen and the unseen and you are *both.* That shit you tried to work on him? It didn't stand a chance."

Echo, I'm tired of looking at her face. Are you calling the police or nah? Because I've got shit to do in the morning." I voice.

"Nope. I think we can just let her sit here for a while to think about what she's done. Wood, put that sock back in her mouth and get her a fresh piece of duct tape. Gigi and I are going to stay here for the night."

"Stay here? What do you mean? Where are we supposed to sleep?"

"In the bed, Girl. There's a whole-ass apartment on the other side of this wall. Come on, Sweetness, let me give you a tour. It's got a huge bedroom with a California king bed, bathtub, shower, kitchen...literally everything. This is my home away from home, so I made it comfortable as possible. I designed this whole building, and had it built the way I wanted. Oh, and my mama came in and added her touch too. But yeah...good night, Giselle.

We'll check on you in the morning. And don't even think about trying to get loose. You'll hurt yourself. Besides, even if you did get free, there's no way out, so your ass will still be right here when the police come."

"The both of you can go to hell and suck my—"

Sock in.

Duct tape on.

Before she could finish.

"I'm so glad you said there's a bed and a bathtub here. I'm tired, and I think a shower would do us both some good," I say loud enough to make sure she hears me.

Chapter Thirty-Six

Entering the apartment side of the warehouse, I'm amused. It's set up exactly like the bottom floor of the townhouse, right down to the corner where Sheba used to lay her head. It feels like home.

Making my way to the bedroom, then into the bathroom, I begin to undress, he follows me. I turn the shower to a medium-hot temperature because I remember how he used to complain that I was trying to burn the skin off his body. Once we get it just right, we both hop in.

I begin to cleanse myself, focusing heavily on my pussy and ass because I know he's about to sop me up like a two-piece and a biscuit and I am more than ready. I've been waiting for this.

If he were someone new, I'd have him wait at least four months just to smell the pussy, but Echo didn't have to wait for shit. I've been celibate for the last three years, and I have a feeling we're about to try to make up for that.

Looking down at his body, my nipples perk up, standing out like two chocolate gumdrops. He leans down and takes one into his mouth, gently playing with the other.

"Ooh, yesss," I purr.

His touch is magical. He slides his hand down, past my belly button, and dives into my center with his middle finger. Then he begins circling my clit, and I'm losing it.

I haven't been touched like this in so long that it feels euphoric. He takes my tongue into his mouth and gently sucks on it while still stimulating my clit. I can tell I'm close, so I stop him. I turn the shower off, hop out, and pat myself dry. He follows suit.

Sashaying over to the bed, I sit down, and he gently pushes me back. Biting my ankles and adorning my body with soft kisses has me trembling.

He makes his way up my legs until he reaches the mound of pussy he's been waiting on.

A soft lick sends shivers down my spine.

"Oooohh, yes, Echo. Please make me cum. I need this so bad," I beg.

He devours me, and the moans that escape my mouth almost frighten me.

"Gigi, your pussy tastes so good. I want to drink every drop of you."

He flicks his tongue, licking and sucking until I become breathless and cream right into his mouth. Shrieking, clit tender to the touch, I decide to return the favor.

"Stand up," I tell him.

He follows instructions. Dropping to my knees, I caress his swollen dick and lick the tip of his shaft. He throws his head back, preparing for the ride this tongue is about to take him on.

I take him into my mouth, sucking him slowly, licking up and down while cuffing his balls. I swirl my tongue around his shaft until I hear his toes pop.

"Gigi, baby... that shit feels so good. I've missed you so much...your energy, your body, your mouth," he moans.

The louder he gets, the louder the muffled cries from the other room become.

"Yes, Gigi. Suck that muthafucka...make it disappear."

I lean my head all the way back to accommodate his size. Once my throat is relaxed, I pull his hips toward me, making him fuck my throat. Looking up at him as I gag on his dick has him mesmerized. He grabs the back of my head as he's about to release, and I pull back.

"I want you in me, Echo. I want to feel you in me," I say, pushing him down on the bed and climbing on top of him.

Sitting on his face, I swipe my pussy lips across his nose and down to his sweet mouth. He sticks out his tongue, and I rock back and forth until my nectar starts to drown him. His nose, mouth, and chin glisten with proof of my pleasure.

I slide down to his dick and inch my way down on it until it disappears.

"Fuckkk, Gigi. Fuck."

Riding him slowly, I place my hands on his chest and bounce while grinding my clit against his groin.

"Shiiit, I can't hold it anymore, Gigi. I can't!!"

I bounce faster, grabbing my ankles for leverage, and ride him until we both explode. My pussy milks every drop from him.

"Please stop moving, Gigi. I'm begging you. Girl, I swear I'm about to cry. You know I'm a tender dick ass nigga after I cum. Just stay still and don't move."

I look down at him, smile and glance out the window to see the soft glow of the moonlight. We find ourselves wrapped in each other's arms again. By now, the outside world has faded away and only he and I exist in this time.

I trace the line of his jaw. My fingertips lingering where the roughness of his stubble meets the smoothness of his skin. His eyes soften as he pulls me closer. His lips brushing against mine. Slowly, deliberately until our tongues dance again.

"I've missed this, Gigi," he whispers between kisses. His voice low and intimate, filling with a longing that had built up over time.

"I never want to be without you again, Echo." I whisper back, running my hands through the waves of his hair. Every touch feels like the first time. I realize that our love is simple but profound, not one of burning desire because it is far deeper than that, but a steady flame that warms us both.

We move together, unhurried, savoring the feeling of being whole in each other's arms again. We were meant to be together always. As we finally pull away, our foreheads rest together, our hearts beating in sync.

"We will never be apart again. Promise me that you love me and will never leave me," he whispered. I smile, now knowing that it is a love that would and could last through anything. He's been my everything for so long and I finally had my everything back.

"I love you and I promise," I whisper, my hands tracing the curvature of his chest, feeling the steady rise and fall of his heart beneath my fingertips. We hold each other close. The only thing I could think of that was more perfect than our love and this moment...was the peace of us simply being together again.

Chapter Thirty-Seven

The next morning, I wake up to the sounds of drills and compressors shrieking in my ears.

For a moment, I forget where I am. Then it hits me, I'm still at the shop. Checking my phone, I see it's 7:02 A.M., and today is the day the movers arrive. Echo isn't laying beside me, so I assume he's out there with his crew.

Last night was beautiful, a perfect ending to an extremely shitty day.

I turn my thoughts to Giselle. I don't hear any mumbling through the wall, and I'm scared to assume what that means.

I get up and head to Echo's closet to find something to wear. But being that he's so much taller than me, I already know this isn't going to be easy. If it were spring or summer, a T-shirt and shorts would do, but it's October. It's chilly, and I need something warm.

In the corner of his closet, I spot a box labeled **"My Forever."**

Assuming it holds some of Giselle's things, I'm surprised to find the contents actually belong to me. When I left for basic training, I'd told Echo to donate my things to charity. I thought he did, but I'm pleasantly surprised to find my favorite pajama set, my fuzzy slippers, and a few outfits he bought me when we first met.

Why would he keep these?

I hear a voice behind me. "Ahhh, I see you found it. I was just coming in here to tell you I had some of your stuff. I always knew you'd come back to me. I didn't know when or how, but I knew. I brought that box from the townhouse to the shop because Giselle had a bad habit of going through my shit. I didn't want her to find your stuff and destroy it, so I brought it here, somewhere safe. Guess it wasn't a bad idea after all. See, Gigi? Divine timing is everything."

Smiling, I ask, "Where's Giselle?"

"Oh, she's still in there. I stood her up and let her use the bathroom in a bucket. I gave her milk and bread, too. She might as well get used to eating like that because I believe thats the kind of shit they feed the inmates."

He walks over and plants a big, wet kiss on my lips.

"Did you talk to her? Like, did she say anything to you?"

"Yeah. I took that nasty-ass sock out her mouth so she could eat, and she started saying all kinds of vile and disgusting things about both of us. Apparently fucking and making someone listen is the worst thing that you can do to someone. Not stalking, robbing, battery, assault, fraud, scamming, harassing, or even attempted murder in the state of California, but *fucking*. That's where she draws the line."

We burst out laughing.

"Well, if it makes her feel any better, please kindly let her know that we only fucked once, the second time and third time, we made love. Anyway, enough of her. I'm so excited Echo, today's the big day," I affirm. "The movers should be at the Airbnb in a few hours, so I need to head back over there and grab what I can salvage."

"Okay, I'll go with you, but how about we handle this business with Giselle first? Call that Olufemi dude and let him know we solved his case for him. Tell him to come get the suspect and lock her ass up...so *we* can move on with our lives."

"My pleasure," I say with a grin.

I place a call to Olufemi and give him the address to the shop, telling him Giselle was caught splashing gasoline all over the building and had to be restrained to prevent her from fleeing. I leave out the part where she was gagged with a nasty sock, tied up with mechanic towels, and forced to hear the beautiful sounds of *her* man's love-making skills and the pleasure sounds of the woman receiving them. That's strictly "need-to-know" info and Olufemi, definitely doesn't need to know.

He tells me that he'll gather his team and be here in no less than twenty minutes.

Echo and I hop in and out the shower and get dressed. I look like a comfortable blast from the past, but I don't care. I'm moving into my new house today, and nothing's going to mess that up for me.

I call Angel to let her know what's going on and ask her to pass my workload on to someone else for a week or so. I've got too much going on.

She already knew everything. Her brother told her. News travels fast in Roseville.

Roseville PD pulls up and *shows out.* You would've thought El Chapo was hiding in the damn mechanic shop. They show up with a SWAT team, a couple of U.S. Marshals, and more on the way. According to Olufemi, she's wanted in several states for multiple crimes and will be extradited to California, where the attempted murder charge originated. The attempted murder charge didn't show up in the Roseville PD system until one of their officers used facial recognition and she popped up. Echo knew all of this because he had one of his techie friends run a deep search on her this morning, right before he fed her that slop.

Homegirl's going away for a long time.

Once everything is handled with her, we take the Monte Carlo back to my Airbnb and throw whatever's salvageable into trash bags. All the boxes are soaked. I don't even have the energy to replace them. What we can save fits into three bags. I then call the moving company to confirm that **8379 Sunshine Drive** is the address that they have on file.

I also call the local movers I hired to help with the Airbnb move and let them know I no longer need their services..but I pay them anyway.

I ask Echo about Sheba, and he goes to pick her up from his mother's house. That's where she stays most of the time anyway, since he's always working. Now she'll have *three* homes to visit.

Echo and I spend the next three months making love, shopping for more furniture and household items, making love, decorating, landscaping, making love, organizing what I already have, making love some more and celebrating the holidays together.

In early January, Echo decides to surprise his mom. He gives her my address and tells her to check out this house he's "thinking about buying."

She shows up, and I answer the door.

She's shocked and overjoyed to see me. It feels good to know she still cares for me. She hugs me for five straight minutes and tells Echo she's going to beat his ass for surprising her like that.

She tells me she missed me and how happy she is that I came back to Roseville. Mama Black confesses that she never liked Giselle and always believed Echo and I were meant to be.

She also tells me she was hurt that I'd been back for months and didn't come see her.

I explain, "I told Echo I wanted to come visit, but I needed to get the house and my life situated first."

"I could use your touch, Mama Black. No one decks out a house like you."

"Well, you let me know where I'm needed, babydoll, and I'll see what I can do."

Standing in the foyer, Echo grins from ear to ear.

"Look at my two favorite ladies...back together again. Awww, I think I'm gonna cry."

We all burst out laughing.

Chapter Thirty-Eight

Echo and I are back in the groove of things. It doesn't take long at all. It's as if we've never been apart. After work, he either comes over to my house or I head over to his. Who cooks depends on who had the easier day. Sometimes, between showings, I'll stop by the shop and chill with him until my next appointment. If he has a slow day, he'll bring me lunch or just stop by to see me.

In between all of that, I still manage to visit the school once a week to meet with Mrs. Graham and organize a fundraiser for my nonprofit. Everything is going well with the planning, and we decide to launch the campaign in the spring of next year.

Outside of those meetings, I spend most of my free

time with Echo. Things were splendid until I have a dream that my mother passes away.

When I wake up, I know it's time. I'm ready. I call Echo at work.

"Hey, babe, I need to ask you something."

"Go ahead, baby, but be quick. I'm trying to calibrate this transmission on this foreign, and it's giving me hell."

"Okay. What time do you think you'll be done today?"

"Around six. Why?"

"Can you come earlier? I want to ride over to Whispering Oaks to see my mother. I had a bad dream… and I think it's time."

He hangs up without another word and is at my house minutes later, arriving just as I'm stepping out of the shower. He slaps my ass and gives me the pep talk I didn't know I needed, reminding me that I can do this and that he'll be standing right outside the door if I need him.

"I don't know what I'd do without you, Echo. I truly don't."

"And my prayer is that you never have to find out. We're intertwined, remember? Connected. You are mine, and I am yours. You're my soulmate," he says, kissing the back of my hand.

He heads back downstairs, and I make my way to the closet to get dressed. The thing is huge and so disorganized that finding anything feels impossible. As I dig around for something specific, I come across a box I don't remember packing. It must be mine because I see silk fabric poking out from the corner.

Inside is the dress, purse, and shoes I wore the night of my birthday party. As I lift the dress from the box, the purse falls and a small box tumbles to the floor.

My heart skips. I remember that night. Echo walked me to the car, and a box was waiting in the front seat. He told me not to open it until later. I must have tossed it in my purse and forgotten about it.

Still naked, I sit on the floor, holding the box in my hands, suddenly nervous. Why didn't he remind me to open it? Why did he never mention it again?

"Echo!" I yell.

He appears in the doorway and sits beside me.

"So, you finally remembered, huh? I was wondering if you'd ever get to open that thing."

"Echo, I'm sorry. I completely forgot. I don't think I ever wore that dress and purse again, and I definitely don't remember boxing it up."

"That's because you didn't. I packed it shortly after you left. I thought you'd come back during your military leave, but you never did. So I held onto it. It was at the warehouse. I brought it over a few days ago while you were at work."

"Now you've got me scared. What's in it?"

"Gigi, if I haven't told you in all this time, what makes you think I'm going to tell you now? I figured when the time was right, you'd find it."

"Divine timing," we say in unison, cracking up.

I open the box. Inside is a small piece of paper, folded neatly. Underneath it... a diamond ring.

I stare at it, then at Echo. Tears form in my eyes and fall without permission.

Through the tears, I manage to whisper, "Echo, were you going to propose to me?"

"I think it's time you read the letter, Gigi."

Dear Gigi,

I was going to write you a long, drawn-out letter explaining my love for you, but I don't think it's necessary because I show you every day. I love you more than I ever thought I could love anyone. I know you said that we were young and had our whole lives ahead of us but I don't want to spend any part of my life without you. You are everything to me. You'd make me the happiest man in the world if you'd be my wife. Please accept this ring as a token of my love and honor to you.

Love, Echo

"You mean to tell me... all this time I could've been your wife? That all I had to do was open the damn box?"

"Now that we're older, I think we both know things happened exactly how they were supposed to. You needed to find your own strength, your own way. And I needed to get my shit together. We've both done that. And now, here we are."

"Do you still, Echo?"

"Do I still what, Gigi?"

"Want me to be your wife? Because I'll put this ring on right damn now."

"Of course, the offer still stands. We still standing, ain't we? Hell, I'm already on the floor. You gotta know I really love you...I'm on both knees. Gigi, I've been a simp for your ass from the very beginning."

I burst into laughter.

"See, this is why I could never stop loving you, girl. Look at that smile. That laughter. That beauty. I need that in my life." He leans in, kisses me, and takes the ring from the box.

Sliding it onto my finger, he asks, "Genevieve Melania Parker, will you make me the happiest man in the world and be my wife?"

"Yes. You damn right I will," I say, and the closet erupts with laughter.

"Good. Now get your ass up," he says, helping me off the floor. "Get dressed. Let's go see your mama."

He runs downstairs like nothing just happened.

I scream into my hands, *I'm engaged. I am fucking engaged*!!!

Chapter Thirty-Nine

I gather myself, pick out a nice work outfit because after this visit, duty still calls. Echo and I head out. We drive separately so he can return to work afterwards. Parking before I do, he heads over to open my car door. I step out, confidence radiating from me, as we walk hand-in-hand into the building. I request two visitor passes and we trek down the hallway.

At her door, I stop. Echo nods and mouths, "You got this."

I enter. My mother sits in a reclining chair, watching TV and I sit on the edge of the bed. She doesn't move. Doesn't even look at me. I look back at the door. Echo mouths again; "Just start talking, baby."

"Hey Mama, it's good to see you."

She turns slowly, eyes widening. "Wait a minute... am I dreaming? Nurse! Nuuurse!"

A nurse enters. "What do you need, Miss Parker?"

"I need you to tell me, am I seeing what I think I'm seeing? Is there a lady sitting at the end of my bed?"

"Yes ma'am. And she's beautiful. Looks a lot like you."

"So I'm not seeing shit?"

"No, Miss Parker. Not this time," she laughs.

The nurse asks, "Is this the woman that you keep seeing?"

"Yes, that's her. That's my daughter. My only child. I named her Genevieve after my mama. She's a sweet girl but I didn't do right by her. Not at all. No ma'am. I didn't do right by her at all."

The nurse looks at me, winks, pats my shoulder, and exits.

"Mama, you said... you've been seeing me?"

"Yes, Gigi. I see you all the time. Sometimes I'm dreaming, sometimes I'm not. I can't tell anymore which is which, so I have to ask. You're so pretty, baby girl. So beautiful."

"Thank you, Mama."

"They say my mind's a little bad from the drinking and all that other stuff. But I remember enough. I remember you," she smiles. "I'll never forget you."

"You've got dementia, Mama?"

"That's what they say. I don't know if I believe 'em."

She pauses.

"Where you been all these years. I looked for you, you know. After you left. I got clean. Took me a few months, but I went looking. Guess you were already gone. Where did you go?"

"I graduated high school and joined the military. Ten years served. I just came back a few months ago. I'm a realtor now. I sell houses."

"That's nice, baby. Real nice. You were always so smart. Way smarter than I was."

"Mama, I didn't come to stay long. Just wanted to tell you... I forgave you a long time ago. For all of it. Doesn't matter if you remember. I'm okay now."

"I guess I could sit here and lie and act like I don't remember, but I do. I remember everything, baby. I wasn't doing right by you, Gigi. I was sick. That's not an excuse, but it's the truth. I was a bad mother."

She pauses again, eyes filling with tears.

"I'm sorry. From the bottom of my heart. You didn't deserve that. You didn't deserve me. You probably would have had a better life if I'd given you up for adoption but because I was selfish, I kept you and mistreated you. All because I was hurting inside. And for that, I'm sorry.

You need to know this. Gigi, I was in love with your daddy. And I mean in love. I would have kissed the ground that man walked on. When you were just two years old, he got drunk and took off down the road. The next morning, they found him out in one of those fields, dead. Someone killed him. They took the only man that I've ever loved away from me.

After your daddy died, I couldn't love you the way that I wanted to. I tried but I just couldn't. I didn't even love myself anymore. I was depressed and I started drinking, putting that stuff up my nose and taking those pills to numb the pain. That led to all kind of strife in my life and in turn, I sewed it into yours.

I did you wrong baby and I think about it all the time. I need you to know that none of it was your fault and I don't expect nothing from you because I never gave you nothing. If you left me right now and never came back to see me again, I'd understand but I hope you do come back, and I hope you let me see my grandbaby."

"Grandbaby," I giggle through the tears. "Mama, I'm not pregnant and I don't have any kids."

"That's not what God said."

"So Mama, you know God now?"

"Gigi, you know who my mama was. I've always known God. I just chose to stop listening to him. But don't you worry, I listen now. I can hear him clear as day."

"Mama, I think that it is time for me to go. I have to go to work, but I will stop by and see you from time to time ok. I want to thank you for apologizing to me. You just don't know how much that means to me and I accept it wholeheartedly."

We smile. We embrace. She rubs my stomach and tells me that it's a boy.

"A boy huh, are you sure?"

"You trying to call God a lie?"

"No ma'am. I just didn't know. That's all."

"Now that you are back, maybe you will let me have a chance to do it right this time. I didn't do right by you, and I know it, but I would never do anything to hurt you again. Or that precious baby that you are carrying.

Pastor helped me get rid of those bad spirits a long time ago. I don't wrestle with the same things that I used to anymore. You don't have to make up your mind right now. I want you and your husband to think about it. Tell him I can't wait to meet him okay, Gigi."

"Mama, I'm not married."

"Yeah, but I see that ring so you will be."

"Okay Mama," I say as we embrace. "I'll come back to see you ok."

"And I will be waiting on you Genevieve."

As I WALK OUT of the room, Echo is waiting with open arms.

"You did it, girl. See? Not as bad as you thought," he says, giving me the biggest hug ever.

Standing there stunned, I admit, "I'm confused. I thought she'd deny everything. But she didn't. She owned it. All of it."

"Gigi, sometimes your absence is what people need to see clearly. And you heard her, right? The baby thing?"

"Oh, I heard her, and I know that you also heard her say that she hears and sees things that aren't there."

"Well, I believe her because I shoot your club up every chance I get. I'm talking about in it. Straight machine gun action," he laughs and does a little jig. "Babe, I know that you've got to go to work but I will have the test waiting on you when you get home."

"Boy, stop with your silly tail." I chuckle. "Ain't nobody pregnant. I feel fine. I think that maybe it was wishful thinking on her part."

"Her part *and* mine," he smirks. "We will see.

Chapter Forty

We saunter out of the building, and I feel ten feet tall and lighter than I have in a long time. Echo hugs and kisses me goodbye before hopping in his ride and heading back to work. I sit in the parking lot for another thirty minutes, reflecting on the conversation I had with my mother. I still can't believe she's in a nursing home. All that drinking, smoking, and pill-popping has taken a serious toll on her body.

I thought I'd be furious when I saw her, but I'm not. I told her I was good, and for the first time in my life, I can say it and truly mean it. I've come to terms with my past, because I know it made me who I am today. Her apology wasn't required, but it damn sure helped.

She still seems very cognizant and alert, so I do believe

what she says. Everything except the pregnancy part. I mean, how would she know?

I pull out of the parking lot feeling liberated and ready to tackle the rest of my day. I've got four showings scheduled, so I head to the first house to get started.

By the time I make it to the last showing, I'm exhausted. My head and feet hurt, and I'm more than ready to go home.

When I arrive, I find Echo in the kitchen, whipping it up. He's got a full spread laid out... crab legs, lobster tails, mussels, shrimp, Cajun boiled eggs, potatoes, corn, sausage, and my favorite lemon garlic butter sauce. I'm in heaven. Seafood is my jam.

"Now what did I do to deserve all of this?" I ask.

"Well, the first thing you did was walk in here looking like a goddamn goddess. The second thing you did was one of the hardest things you've ever had to do in your life and baby, you did it with such grace and poise. I had to do something for you."

"That's so sweet, Echo."

"I am proud of you, Gigi. That couldn't have been easy seeing your mother in that condition or even talking to her like that. But you did it like the boss you are."

"That's right, baby, hype me up 'cause I'm *that bitch*," I say, walking to the kitchen island and giving my man a big, sloppy kiss.

"Now sit down, girl. I've got your tray right here and it's ready to go. Your butter is in that bowl over there, and the big cutting shears are next to you. I want you to be careful with these king claws. They're sharp. If you need me to get the meat out, just let me know."

"Echo, I'm not a baby. I can open my own crabs and get the meat out. I get your meat out without any help. Don't I?"

"Stop being nasty. Oh, and speaking of babies, here you go," he says, handing me a CVS bag full of pregnancy tests.

"Are we still on this, Echo?" I giggle as I crack my crab legs.

"Since you won't leave it alone, I'll take it. But it'll be after I finish eating. Where's my fur baby?"

"I put her in her crate. This house is still kind of new to her, and she peed on the living room floor. You know our baby's older than Methuselah. Good thing you've got marble floors."

"You know I hate when you say things like that, right?" I tease.

"This is your house too. Say *our floors not your floors.*"

"Gigi, stop playing with me. Oh, and I've got another surprise for you. But I'll give it to you after you finish eating."

"Okay, good. I'm starving, and I don't think I could stop now even if I wanted to."

The food is delicious, and I'm stuffed. All I want to do is nap, but I know if I sleep now, I won't sleep tonight so I keep myself awake. I put the food away, clean the kitchen, and then attempt to organize my closet. It's a mess, and I can't live like this.

Echo enters the room with the CVS bag, singing *"It's time"* in his best Mariah Carey voice.

Frustrated, I snatch the bag out of his hands and march into the bathroom. I can't wait to prove him and my mother wrong.

With all the sodium from the seafood, I've already had about four glasses of water, so peeing isn't going to be a problem.

I open three separate pregnancy tests, sit on the toilet, and pee on the ends of all three. I set them on the counter, wash my hands, and go back to my closet.

Echo eagerly awaits the results while lying across the bed, cracking his fingers.

"Are you nervous, Echo? Because with all that cracking in there, it sounds like you're nervous."

"No, I don't think I'm nervous. I think I'm just anxious. You've been in that closet for like five minutes now, so I know those tests are ready."

"Well then go look at them. I'm busy and you could be

helping me in here instead of worrying about a doggone test."

"Babe!" he yells.

"Yes, my love?"

"We need to get your mama a Ms. Cleo deal cause she was on point. Whooooo hooooooo! Yeah, nigga, yeah! Yeeeeesssssss Gigi! You is my baby mamaaa! I'm is your baby daddyyyy! We is gonna have a babyyyy!" he sings, laughing joyfully.

"Shut up, Echo! Are you serious?!?!" I ask as I jump up and run to the bathroom.

He's holding the test in his hand, and all I see is:

PREGNANT – 1-3 MONTHS.

I am *floored.*

Chapter Forty-One

Echo has the biggest shit-eating grin I've ever seen. He runs over to me, picks me up, and kisses me like he means it. Gently, he places me back on the floor and grabs his phone and places a Face-Time call.

"Hey Mama, where's Dad and Stormy?"

"They're in the kitchen frying fish and making potato salad."

"Can you take your phone and go in there with them? I've got something I want to show y'all."

"Okay, son. Hold on a minute. I'm walking in there now."

"Echo, noooo," I whisper. "We're supposed to wait at least three months before we tell anybody."

"Girl, ain't nobody worried about that. This is God's doing. We're gonna be alright."

"Okay, Son, we're all here. What is it?"

He holds the pregnancy test in front of the phone.

His mother screams. His sister looks shocked, and his dad just smiles, looking proud.

"Congratulations, y'all!"

"Thank you, Mama," we say in unison.

Then Echo grabs my left hand and throws my ring finger in front of the camera. They scream again, and we both crack up laughing.

"I'm so happy for the two of y'all! Finally, we get a grand-baby, *and* a new daughter. Now we've got to go celebrate. Bye!" His mama hangs up, still screaming with joy.

Echo picks me up again, spins me around, and drops to his knees to kiss my stomach.

"Hey, you in there... Lil man, I know you're just a peanut right now, but your mama and daddy got big things poppin' out here. You're going to have so much love around you, you won't ever want for nothing. You've got an amazing grandmother and grandfather who can't wait to meet you. A precocious auntie who's dying to boss you around. Plenty of mechanic uncles. And another grandma who predicted you before we even knew. We're definitely going to let her meet you someday."

"Ain't that right, baby?" he asks, looking up at me.

"Right. I'll let my mom meet him or her, but I've got to think on it. My therapist told me a long time ago that forgiveness doesn't require reconciliation. I can forgive her and keep my distance. I waited a long time for that moment, and I'm glad I made peace with it. But I'm not going to rush anything with her.

Truthfully, I don't know if I'll ever be comfortable enough to let anyone else take my baby out of my sight. I already don't trust a soul except you. With a baby… it's about to be ten times worse!! Lord, let me get my therapist on the line because this right here is a whole different ball-game," I say with a nervous laugh.

"Babe, I told you earlier I had a surprise for you and this time, I won't let you forget. I'll be right back."

"Echo, you're always doing something. Why can't you just sit your ass down somewhere? I know you've never been diagnosed, but ain't nobody gonna tell me that you don't have ADHD," I giggle.

"Whatever," he says while darting out the room.

I hear the door open and close. Within minutes, he's back in my face, handing me an envelope.

"What is this, Echo?"

"Girl, stop asking all those questions. Just open it."

"Okay, dang." I open it. It's a letter from my mortgage lender, confirming that my loan has been paid in full. Not only do I now own my house and the land it's on, but also the three vacant lots beside and behind it.

I stand up and hug Echo as tightly as I can.

"Boy, this house was almost two million dollars and you paid it off and bought more land?! Why did you do that?"

"It just made sense, Gigi. Don't you know you deserve it? I did this last week, before we even knew about the baby. I'm glad I did. Especially now that we've got a little one on the way and we're about to jump the broom. Plus... I love this house."

"So why haven't you moved in yet, Echo?"

"Shiddd, because you haven't asked me. Didn't I ask you to come stay with me?"

"Echo Ezra Black... will you do me the honor of moving in with me?"

"Hell yeah, I will! I'm moving my shit in tomorrow!" He does a little jig, and I burst out laughing.

"I guess it's time to put my townhouse up for rent. That'll be some extra change for us.

Gigi, since you don't have a mortgage anymore. You don't have anything to worry about. You know I've got all the bills. I have a feeling you're going to be a helicopter mama. This way you won't have to stress about finding a babysitter. You can quit your job—"

I side-eye him.

"Only if you want to, of course. You can stay home with our little munchkin. I just want you happy and stress-free. This is a good start, isn't it?"

"Echo, you're always so thoughtful and three steps ahead of everybody. If I didn't love and trust you like I do, I would've said hell no to everything you just said. But... you're right. I do want to be at home with *my* babies."

"Aht! You said *babies*. So you *do* want more than one. Perfect. I want at least six!"

"Ion know about all that. Six babies out of *whose* cooda cat? Can't be mine. I was thinking two or three. Six is *crazy*. I'd lose my mind, Echo."

"Okay, baby, we'll compromise. How about four?"

"I can't with you," I laugh. "Can we just get this one out first before we plan the family reunion?"

"Seriously though," I continue. "Thank you again for everything. I feel like I'm always thanking you. I need to step my game up. What can *I* do for *you*, Echo? What do *you* need?"

"I've got it, Gigi. God gave me you and a seed. That's more than I could've ever asked for. All I need now is to upgrade that ring and set a wedding date."

"I'm leaving the planning to your mama. I know she's gonna knock it out of the park. I think I'll go with blush pink, gold, and ivory. And don't say shit about my colors, Echo. You look great in pink."

"Do you think we can get a little session in before bed? I heard pregnant cat is the best cat," he says while pinching my nipple and biting my ear.

"Boy, you been getting this pregnant cat all along. What are you even talking about?"

"Thing is, I didn't *know* it was pregnant cat. Now that I do, it's gonna be even better."

"Echo," I say, giggling. "Please unass my titty. And no coochie for you until we go to the doctor. I don't want that big ol' donkey dick messing anything up. I need to make sure everything's okay before we keep hunching."

"Damn, Gigi. We're not even married yet and you're already rationing out the coochie."

"Don't worry, babe. You won't be waiting long. I'm calling the doctor first thing in the morning to make an appointment. Are you coming with me?"

"You know I am. I wouldn't miss it for the world. I'm not missing *anything* that has to do with you or my seed. You're my everything, girl. I'm never leaving your side again."

THE END

Epilogue

And he didn't. He kept his promise. Every one of them.

Echo was there every step of the way. Our due date was September 29. We chose not to find out the gender. I wanted it to be a surprise. Once I received my due date, I knew I didn't want to walk down the aisle big and pregnant and Echo didn't want to wait another second. "The quicker, the better," he said.

We had a small, beautiful wedding in his parents' backyard. It was perfect. Mrs. Black did her thing, just like always.

I didn't have many guests from my side, but that was fine with me. I've always been a loner. Angel came as my maid of honor, and my mother, three coworkers, and two of my former teachers were there. Echo had damn near the whole city behind him.

Our son, Divine Love Black, was born *on* his due date—September 29 at 10:28 p.m. He was the most beautiful thing I'd ever laid eyes on. The moment they placed him in my arms, I was smitten. A mama's boy already.

Echo's an amazing father, just like I knew he would be. He extended all the love and care he'd given me, to our son. We're a happy family of three and currently working on baby number two.

I moved my mother to a better facility and introduced her to her grandson. Six months later, she passed away. Echo and I planned a heartwarming memorial. Only one person showed up...Rolla.

I laid my mother to rest next to my grandmother.

Before my mother died, she gave me my father's full name. I've since connected with the family I never knew existed. I have uncles, aunts, cousins, and even a grandmother. Many of them I already knew, but I didn't know we were blood. They welcomed me with open arms and we are building relationships little by little. I actually have relatives!

Echo has been working hard, like always. My baby's a true hustler. We're breaking ground on two more auto restoration/mechanic shops. Since getting married, we've acquired two more investment properties and are searching for a third.

I took Echo up on his offer. I'm officially a stay-at-home mom. I still have my real estate license, but now I manage the backend for our businesses from home. My nonprofit, *Black's Better Tomorrow*, is thriving. Our first fundraiser raised $182,000 for children in need. My mother-in-law and cousins helped me plan it. It was everything I dreamed it would be.

Children need to know that there are people out there that care. That there are people who will help them...without expecting anything in return. Someone cared enough to help me and I wanted to pay it forward in a major way. I never thought that I'd be where I am in life but I'm here and doing just fine.

I attend therapy twice a month. Having a child made me want to become the best version of myself. I refuse to let the toxicity I experienced, bleed into my children's lives so I do everything possible to prevent that from happening.

Healing doesn't look the same for everyone and it's not linear.

Some people can heal alone. Not me. I needed help. Echo's love played a massive part in putting the pieces of my broken heart back together.

I'm in the best mental space I've ever been in.

I'm somebody's wife.
I'm a mother.
I'm a boss.
I'm a motivator.
I'm a business owner.
And I am officially **THAT BITCH**.

About the Author

L.L. Momon is a passionate storyteller who crafts emotionally rich, character-driven novels that explore healing, love, and resilience. Born and raised in Tuskegee, Alabama, and now residing in Florida, Momon brings Southern warmth and depth to every story she writes.

A nail technician by trade and an intuitive introvert at heart, she draws inspiration from the complexities of real-life relationships and personal growth. As a wife and mother, she deeply values the strength of family, and that love radiates through the pages of her work.

With five published novels to her name, including her

latest, *To Love the Broken and Unhealed*, L.L. Momon is known for delivering raw, honest stories centered on strong, imperfect Black characters navigating trauma, passion, and redemption.

When she's not writing, you'll find her creating beauty with her hands, enjoying quiet moments with her family, cooking up soul-soothing meals, or binge-watching her favorite TV shows. Through every story, L.L. Momon reminds readers that even the most broken hearts are capable of healing and that love, when nurtured, is a force worth believing in.

instagram.com/authoresslImomon
facebook.com/authorllmomon
tiktok.com/authoresslImomon
amazon.com/author/llmomon

Also by L L Momon

Whittling Wood

Whittling Wood 2

A Savage and Her Wicked Wats

A Savage and His Lying Tongue

www.ingramcontent.com/pod-product-compliance
Lightning Source LLC
Chambersburg PA
CBHW031225020726
47499CB00002B/644